Death Dresses Poorly

by Marc Watson

I hope you enjoy
my depressing book!

Marc Watson

FLUKY FICTION
Newport, ME

Death Dresses Poorly
by Marc Watson
Print Edition ISBN: **978-0-9987173-4-0**

Published by Fluky Fiction

WWW. FLUKYFICTION. COM

For Jen, who has to live with every jerk in this book

Chapter 1

He sat quietly in his chair, trying not to think about the last few days. He had loved her once, but those years were long gone, and now, so was she.

His hand barely had a grip on the tablet on his lap. Mindless videos played on repeat, but he barely saw them. As much as he tried to distract himself from where he'd just been, he couldn't. It was simply too hard.

His mother was gone. No chance for redemption. No reconciliation. Their time was up.

It wasn't until he realized that his eyes were getting wet that he snapped out of his funk and looked up. Starting to cry? Unbelievable. He'd written her off ages ago. He was only here as a promise to his sister. Now he could get back to normal, no matter how unimpressive his normal was. Yeah, he wasn't a big success, but he wasn't some drugged-out nut job either, so he had that going for him. Besides, he was only twenty, and last he checked his last name wasn't Zuckerberg or Musk, and he was thankful for it. Successful people could lick his balls. He was living his *own* dream now.

Admittedly, his dream was stupid, but at least it was his.

His brain suddenly started to process the announcements and conversations and white noise all around him. O'Hare was its typical cacophony of over-emotional idiots

1

and douchebag businessmen. He couldn't fucking stand them. Gotta go get somewhere! Heaven forbid the trades weren't made or meetings weren't scheduled or the NASDAQ numbers fell or climbed or whatever it was they had to fucking do to be bad and cause a panic. He didn't know and he didn't care. His portfolio was so diversified that it didn't exist.

It was then that he noticed him. He stood next to the gate agent, talking casually as he turned to look at the seated passengers around him.

Ethan couldn't tell why his eyes were suddenly drawn to him. He wasn't in a suit or anything else he hated. He wasn't handsome or ugly or anything really of note. His hair was sun-bleached blonde beyond what might have been considered normal and was cut like an Eighties over-fifty male Sears catalogue model. His skin was pale and unblemished. Both of these traits stood out against his all-black outfit. Nothing of note. Some prick flying off to see his wife or his mistress or both at the same time. You never knew what someone was into.

As he stepped away from the counter, Ethan quickly turned his eyes down and was thankful for his oversized headphones to throw up the universal signal for "Do Not Disturb". It didn't stop the man from choosing a seat two to his right, facing the same window and staring out to the same overcrowded tarmac, but it probably stopped him from starting an actual conversation. He looked like a talker.

Ethan stole glances at the man, and the more he did, the more this perfectly normal, non-business guy seemed

2

off. His whole ensemble was black. Sport coat, pants, turtleneck, socks, and shoes were all so black that they seemed to absorb light like a 70s velvet picture. The thing that was most off about the getup was that they were all the exact same shade. Ethan had spent enough time as a wallowing, depressed teenager with a druggie mother and deadbeat father that he was well-versed in the various shades of black that clothing could afford. As a teenager, you either knew too much color, or you knew black. He was the latter, and he knew that nothing ever matched this well.

He was so wrapped up in stealing glances at the man to his right that he missed the man on his left, who came much too close for anyone's comfort, and tapped Ethan on the shoulder.

"Jesus shit!" Ethan exclaimed, drawing more than a few startled or offended glances while he ripped his headphones off his ears. "What the fuck, man? Why the fuck are you so close to my face! Back off!"

Ethan then noticed the man's outstretched hand, and was instantly afraid it was a knife or something dangerous. Contrary to popular belief, Ethan had no response to that if it was something harmful. He simply stood there, staring at the hand, wondering why fiction made it seem like all humans had cat-like reflexes when faced with this kind of situation. Nope. He just stared, about to get stabbed or bludgeoned or poisoned like a Russian government defector.

There was no knife. Just a business card he recognized instantly. On one side was a collection of pictures denoting the Sign Language alphabet and on the other was the typical plea for help.

"Hello, I am deaf and mute. Please donate and I and my organization will gift you with this grateful token. Thank you and God bless." The man held out the other hand and showed Ethan a small box filled with what looked like packs of tiny screwdrivers.

Ethan raised his eyebrow skeptically. "Bullshit. What organization?" he asked. He was far too cynical to just take a beggar on faith.

No response; just an expectant stare. *He's mute, idiot, or at least he claims to be. What the fuck did you expect?*

Finally calmed from being scared out of his blissful ignorance, Ethan looked at the box again. Normally he hated charity of any kind, but as fate would have it, he actually was in need of a new glasses screwdriver. He couldn't afford to get a new pair, so he needed to keep repairing the ones he had. *What a happy fucking coincidence.*

Considering where he'd just been and the circumstances that had led to him sitting in this chair right at this moment in time, he decided to be uncharacteristically karmic, pulled a five out of his jeans pocket and handed it to the man.

The man's eyes lit up, and he more or less bowed while making a half-hearted attempt at a sign of the cross with his hands full, followed by snatching the five like a raccoon and quickly tossing the novelty token onto Ethan's lap. Then, he was gone up one of the many twisting corridors of America's busiest airport without propositioning another soul.

4

Ethan picked up the little pack of three colorful screwdrivers and smirked. Why the hell had he done that? He guessed his mother's funeral was the cause of his grand charity.

"I'm sorry," said a clear tenor voice from his right. Ethan was once again startled back into the now. The encounter with the deaf mute had completely distracted him from the odd man in black, and his blessed "Fuck Off" headphone message was now around his neck. Dear God; he was actually exposed to the *public!* Horrifying. There were *idiots* in public! Idiots, assholes, and all manner of other such deplorable people, and he just opened the front door to what he suspected was a huge one.

Oh well. Nothing to be done about it now. "How's that?" Ethan asked back, looking back at the man's unremarkable face. Wait… had he always been wearing wire-framed glasses? How hadn't he noticed that?

The man indicated the direction the deaf mute had toddled off to. "That sneaky beggar. I saw him coming. I should have warned you."

"Warned me? Against what? I imagine I can likely handle some shit-peddling con-artist like that."

"You don't have an imagination. You're what I call the 'screen zombie' generation. It's hilariously tragic."

Ethan suddenly went flush. He was once again unprepared for confrontation, and he just sat there bathing in the insult before realizing that the man likely was right. Had he not been so wrapped up in catching a glimpse at his neighbor, he would have been staring at the tablet, buried in either that or his own mind. Oh well. Time to fire back.

"Yeah, it may be tragic, but it's better than the alternative of having to talk to people. Those invasive fuckers are crazy." He held the man's eyes, hoping he kept his dig ambiguous enough to not just have started another fight he couldn't finish.

Surprisingly, the man looked away and smiled, seemingly not offended. "Damn right they are. Full of ideas and dreams and emotions and whatever. Either way, sorry again. He's likely off using that five for drugs or booze or Taco Tuesday specials or something."

"It's Thursday."

"Is it? Huh. That's a shame. No taco specials on Thursday."

"True. Half-off picnic buckets at KFC, though."

"Oh great," the man laughed, "I was due for a colonoscopy. Better flush those pipes ahead of time. The doctors will appreciate a sparkling clean poop chute."

Ethan was surprised to feel himself smile. The man seemed to share his bleak outlook on the state of fast food in this country.

Ethan turned the little pack of screwdrivers over in his hand. "It's not so bad, honestly. Oddly enough, I needed one of these."

"Who the hell needs teeny tiny screwdrivers?"

"For my glasses, asshole," Ethan shot back defensively.

"Well obviously it's not for your itty bitty Ikea furniture. I just mean don't glasses stores give you all of the useless little tidbits and crap now? Like sprays and wipes and fancy cases with Nolte Cabana on them?"

Ethan shrugged. "Maybe. I haven't bought a new pair in a while. My mom bought me a pair in tenth grade and I've had them ever since."

"Then get your mom to buy you a new pair so you can get that crap and avoid guilt-peddling liars like that guy. Moms are great for shit like that."

"Freshly dead ones aren't," Ethan answered, regretting it immediately. Having a dead mother was a recent development and he wasn't accustomed to the truth yet. He absolutely loathed false sympathy, and he'd just opened himself up to a mountain of it.

"True," replied the man without missing a beat, "but their inheritances are."

The answer shocked Ethan. From the moment this had happened and he'd started telling people why he needed to go back to Chicago, the limited number of people he'd interacted with in that time had been disgustingly saccharine towards him. Coworkers and his loose circle of friends were stepping over themselves to make him feel better and it made his stomach lurch with every attempt.

"I guess. Not much tucked away in the wallet of a drug addict, though." Sweet Christ almighty, why the fuck couldn't he keep his mouth shut?

"Whoa now, that's where you're wrong!" the man replied, again not missing a step. "No one has more loose cash tucked away than an addict. They store it away during lucid times and then get all messed up and forget they ever did it. Pull back a few floorboards and you'll find what you need for a great new pair of Oakleys or Ray-Bans or whatever people wear these days. I haven't bought a pair in a while either. But yeah, just dig a little. Unless she was into some hard stuff like crack or meth. Then I don't have as much hope. You don't look like you were a crack baby, but you never know."

Again, Ethan was taken aback. Conversations about recently deceased mothers weren't supposed to go this way. He couldn't tell if he was disgusted or thankful for a more human conversation.

He never had much time to think about it. The man looked away, and then back slowly. Deliberately. "Well, on that morbid note, I need to be off. So long, kid. Have fun with your Barbie hand tools." He smirked to himself while standing. "Damn, that sounds like a shitty Cosmo sex experiment."

Ethan had no real response, other than suddenly realizing this odd man was leaving. "Wait, isn't this your plane?"

The man put his hands into his black pockets and shook his head. "Oh lord no. Who the hell wants to go to Seattle at this time of year? I just like mingling with the masses while we all play the waiting game."

Ethan raised an eyebrow at him. "That's a pretty sketchy thing to do these days, man."

"It sure is. That's why I do it. Before 9/11 it was so much easier to just hang out in airports and talk. Now, we all need a place to be, and I'm no exception. Besides, now I want a bucket of chicken. So long."

Something inside Ethan welled up, likely from the messed-up emotional state the funeral had put him in. "Hey, man…" he turned back and they looked at each other again, "thanks. For talking to me like a human, I mean."

"Aren't you human? Aren't you a spoiled, under-cultured, uneducated tablet monkey from the 'Me' generation? I figured being aloof and cynical was the only way to talk to you."

"I prefer the term 'social media educated', but you seem close enough."

"Educated seems a stretch, from what I see in the world. Look, sorry about your mother. But not really, right? Since I didn't know her and that's just shit I guess we're supposed to say. Head on home to your rainy city and just roll with what's next."

"Sounds good. What's next?"

"Next you learn about the infinite complexity of the universe."

"Cool. Is there an app for that or something?"

No answer. Just a wave and a final smirk, and off the man vanished into the crowd.

Chapter 2

Ethan stood and wandered into the bathroom, his hospital robe concealing little as he moved. His body ached, his head was pounding, and each step sent a shockwave up the back of his left leg.

He looked at his reflection in the mirror. *Thank God*, he thought, *I still look like shit*.

After the crash he'd been sent to UW Med Center to recover, although he didn't have any life-threatening injuries. He was just happy he hadn't been taken to Virginia Mason. Something about that building gave him the creeps, even though he'd never been inside. Even here, he wasn't keen on a bunch of students working on him if something went wrong, even if they were older, smarter, and more driven than he'd ever be.

It had been three days since the plane back from the funeral in Chicago had suffered a *critical mishap*, overshot SeaTac, and plunged into Puget Sound, missing Vashon Island by only a few hundred yards. Ethan still didn't have any answers as to why the plane went down. Only that the comically inept description of *critical mishap* kept popping up. It wasn't terrorists, though. That meant some other, less intelligent means brought them down. Terrorists at least did shit like that on purpose. Just crashing a plane like this meant some asshole had screwed up. Pilots. Mechanics. Some idiot at Boeing. Was he even on a

Boeing? Why did that matter? There was a sad irony in almost being killed by a plane that was likely built in his newly adopted home town, while being run by an office in his old one. He was just going to assume it was a Boeing. It was darkly funnier that way, and he needed humor.

After taking a piss that was blissfully less painful the more he did it, he wandered back out to his private room (a luxury he likely had the airline to thank for) and stared out the window. In the distance he could make out the cold gray of the sound he'd been found in last Thursday.

He couldn't remember much. He could recall the plane shuddering violently as they started their descent and the panic slowly worming its way through the other passengers. He also remembered himself remaining oddly cool. Maybe it was his mentality at the time, but he seemed to know that he would either be fine and the plane would just land, or he would crash and still be fine. Why did he arrogantly believe he could survive a plane crash? Whatever the reason was, it looked like he was right, and as far as he knew it, he was the only one.

He could remember people screaming as the plane descended towards the water. More than one person seemed calm, citing the Miracle on the Hudson as proof that they had nothing to worry about. Then, the plane banked, the starboard wingtip clipped the water at about 150mph, and everything went to shit.

Ethan remembered the fuselage tearing open in front of him as the body of the plane twisted and cracked. As the rip grew, he saw the outside world spin past as he lurched in the deceleration. His last memory was having the idiotic idea to unclip his seatbelt and jump.

It had apparently worked. He smacked his head on the way out and had suffered a concussion. Because of that, the crash was erased from his memory and it had blurred the following 24 hours. He could remember the hazy image of swimming for a floating chunk of the broken plane nearby, climbing on top of it, and being found by Search and Rescue, cold but alive in that same place a short time later. His brain had thankfully edited out the image of bodies in the water around him, which there almost certainly were.

Since then, in his cushy private room, he'd slowly come to grips with what had just happened. Lawyers and reporters and friends (or as close as he had to friends) had tried to get access to him and he'd turned them all away. He'd only seen doctors and nurses, and for now he wanted to keep it that way. Even his sister had flown in the day before, but he still refused to see her.

Lost in thought once again while he struggled to put it all together, he missed the sound of the door opening.

"Your ass is hanging out, son," someone said, snapping Ethan out of yet another haze. Ethan didn't even turn.

"Well, if that's the worst thing to happen to me today, I'll consider myself lucky."

"Fair enough. Nothing I haven't seen before."

Ethan finally turned after a moment of further silence and saw the face of an older doctor he'd never met. He was balding and wrinkled and seemed to fit the textbook definition of what a senior doctor should look like.

"How are you feeling?" he asked, pulling out the clipboard on the wall and going over whatever it was he saw there. Ethan suspected he wasn't even reading it and was just going through the motions of what a doctor was supposed to do when he walked into a room.

"I feel like I got hit by a plane."

The doctor didn't look up. "Understandable, but humor me."

"Better. It hurts less when I piss, and my head isn't throbbing as much. Pain in my leg when I walk, but nothing I can't deal with."

The doctor made a note. Maybe he really was using the clipboard. "And the nurses tell me you don't want anything heavier than extra strength Advil. We have some stuff that could really help you along that's stronger than that."

Ethan shook his head. "No thanks. I can get by with those."

"Does it have to do with your mother?" Ethan looked at him skeptically. "Don't look so shocked. When you were unresponsive we had to search your family history."

Made enough sense, he guessed. "Well since you like prying so much, yes, as a matter of fact it does. In fact, I was flying back from putting her in the ground as a result of too many of those damn pills meeting a healthy dose of Costco-brand whiskey, so forgive me if I don't jump at the chance to be shot full of opiates."

The doctor suddenly looked embarrassed. "I'm sorry. I really am. I wasn't aware that was the nature of your trip."

Ugh. That sickening false sympathy again. "Save it. You're not actually sorry, and she's better off." It hurt to say that, but he wasn't in a cordial mood.

"Regardless of what you think," the doctor replied, "I am sorry. I can't say I blame you for the dire attitude, all things considered."

"Oh don't be so sure, Doc. I had this attitude long before I crashed into the sound."

Unsure of how to continue the conversation, the doctor opted for a new one. "Yes, well, my name is Dr. Gary Graeme, and I'm Head of Medicine here. I wanted to personally come and see how you were doing. You're our newest celebrity, and I wanted to come and let you know what the plan is going forward once we let you out."

"Wait, am I being discharged? I jumped out of a fucking plane crash!"

"No, not yet. But shortly, yes. There's no need to keep you here longer than necessary, and you're doing remarkably well, according to the charts." He indicated the clipboard, though Ethan was still convinced it was just a prop in his hands. "We need to have a few psychologists and trauma counselors speak to you before we can approve a discharge, and I really doubt you'll get very far without speaking to the lawyers from the airline, but physically there's nothing more we can do for you here that couldn't be done in the comfort of your own home. No serious injuries. No signs of shock, shock-ingly enough..." he paused, hoping his moment of levity was appreciated.

"Ugh. Fucking terrible," Ethan answered to Dr. Graeme's dismay.

"Right, well after a few more quick tests, and a gamut of interviews, you'll be on your way."

"No reporters," Ethan said firmly, clenching his teeth. As someone who hated false sympathy, speaking to the press and making a national spectacle of himself was like entering into every ring of Hell all at once. When one of the nurses had mentioned that it may be a great way to make some money and start fresh in the wake of this tragedy that had claimed one hundred and thirteen lives, Ethan immediately quipped back, "And you think the airline is just going to forget I exist and hope I go away? I'll bet they're printing the check right now."

"No. No reporters, as you requested," Dr. Graeme agreed. "I don't care for them much either. So, can we agree to have a few of our professionals come and speak with you?" Ethan agreed, signed some papers without reading them, and Dr. Graeme left the room and Ethan in silence.

It actually took two days of meetings, interviews, and head shrinking to get to the point where the hospital staff was satisfied that he could begin the discharge process. Ethan couldn't help but notice the looks he got from some of the other patients in the halls. He'd seen *Unbreakable* and read *Harry Potter* years ago and remembered that same scene: people enamored by the boy who lived. The sooner he could get these eyes off of him the better. Ethan and attention were bitter enemies.

It was after one of these walks through the hall that he returned to his room and was startled to find a man looking out his window. He wore a long black trench coat and black Converse All Stars with the stark-white soles. His hands were in his pockets and he seemed to be looking down. There was something familiar about his hair, though: sun-bleached blonde, and long enough to be unfashionable for the times.

Immediately thinking hospital security had gone lax, he turned to leave and get away from this intruder, sure it was a reporter or another lawyer (he'd already met one, as part of the condition of his release). When he left his room, Ethan realized that every hall was empty. There was no one to be found anywhere. The hospital had gone perfectly silent.

"Why the fuck aren't you dead," came a tenor voice that bordered on recognizable. Ethan looked back at the man as he turned from the window, trying to put together what was happening. "Do you have any idea the work I put into that accident? The manipulating and the machinations I had to do to get everything just right? The sacrifices I needed to make just to have you go down? One hundred and thirteen people, Ethan! One hundred and thirteen people who had to die just so I could get my hands on you, and here you fucking are, standing in one of those god-awful robes with your ass hanging out, while one hundred and thirteen people are fish food. I hope you're proud of yourself."

Ethan backed away with every word of the rant, slowly realizing who it was he was speaking to. By the time the man turned all the way around, even with the dreary light of the window behind him, Ethan immediately recognized the face of the man from O'Hare Airport slowly walking towards him. The same matching black ensemble contrasted by his light hair and pale skin.

Ethan had no idea what to say. He was terrified beyond imagination at what he was seeing. Whether it was real or in his head (which was far more likely), he knew this man wasn't supposed to be here.

"You know, I was half-heartedly telling the truth when I said you were an uneducated tablet monkey, but I thought you were different. I thought you were smarter than that. Turns out you're just stubborn. Stubborn and blind."

"What... What the fuck? Who the fuck are you?" Ethan stammered out, hardly paying attention to the man who now stood a few feet away from him in the hallway outside his room. Ethan had unwittingly backed up against the wall and was pressed against it.

"Where's your witty millennial come-back now, eh? Who the hell do you think I am? The God-damned Anti-Pope? I'm Death, you idiot. The Grim Reaper. The Quiet Stranger. The Man at the End of the Path. Horseman Number Four. Bad Hangover Henry. The guy you pray to when you wake up next to some ugly chick to come and take you away after a hard-boozing night. Jesus, how dense are you. Oh wait, scratch that question, because the answer is obviously *very*, or else we wouldn't be having this conversation in the first place!"

"Bull… Bullshit!" Ethan spit out, looking into the ice-blue eyes of the man opposite him. "Seriously, are you a lawyer or something from the airline? I already agreed to meet with you guys after I get home."

The man feigned being stabbed in the heart. "A lawyer? Ouch! You wound me, Ethan. Deeply. Not much worse things you could call a guy." He put his hands back down and became serious again in an instant. "No, thankfully I'm not a lawyer. People like me more than them, anyway."

"Well, then who the fuck are you, and why are you here in Seattle!?"

"Hey, I told you I didn't want to come here. Hell is more appealing than Seattle in February, and a damn site warmer, too. But you had to be Little Ethan Wanna' Live, so here I am. I crashed a plane, kid! Do you think I can manipulate that many innocent lives without consequence? Do you get how much work I had to go through to make sure they all met their death with open realization? I hate plane crashes! They're so messy. That's part of the reason I had it happen in the water. It was worth it to get to you, but I didn't! I don't know how you humans deal with this 'frustration' feeling all the time, but I've had my fill for an eternity."

Ethan's head was racing. This had to be a symptom of the concussion, but damned if it didn't seem real.

The man's eyes started racing, but his body remained unmoving, with his hands firmly in his pockets like he was squeezing something very tightly. "You know what? I'm done with you right now. I have no idea how to deal with this, and I need a drink. Since this is Seattle, what are the odds I can get a regular beer and not some pretentious microbrew crap? Not very good, I'll bet. Go on. Keep doing your *living* thing, and I'll come for you when I calm down."

Ethan looked concerned for a moment as the man's statement sunk in. "Come... come for me? You're going to murder me?"

"Murder is harsh. I prefer 'showing you the universe from the other side'." Ethan started to go white. "Oh, relax. If I could just murder you, this conversation wouldn't be necessary. No, unfortunately you've forced me to have to do this the hard way: interpersonal relationships. Ugh, God, just saying that makes my skin crawl."

Death looked at the door, and then back again. "Look, in a few minutes Dr. Graeme is going to come back with your discharge papers. Do what you need to do, get away from the madness that is the vultures outside the front door, and I'll head off, drink a lot, and figure out another way to convince you to die. We've got work to do and you're just gumming up the works like a toothless hooker. I'll meet you back at your place soon. In the meantime, if you could just try and die, even a little, it would really mean a lot."

Before Ethan could answer, the man waved his arm and was gone without any indication he was ever there. In a rush, the hallway was filled with people who materialized out of nowhere, and the world went from absolute silence to the standard low-volume chaos of a typical hospital. Ethan looked back and forth, shocked at the sudden change, unsure what to make of anything that had just happened. A woman in a wheelchair was across from him outside the door to his neighboring hospital room. "Hey kid, you ok?"

Ethan realized she was talking to him, and he looked at her questioningly. "I have no idea. Was there a man just standing here? A man in black, about my height, with blonde hair and sneakers?"

She looked at him quizzically. "No, son. No one standing out here but you and me. Well, as it were." She indicated her chair. "Like I said, you ok?"

Ethan grasped his eyes and rubbed. He hadn't put his glasses on today and suddenly they hurt like hell. "No, no I'm not. I need to get out of here."

He walked unsteadily towards the door to his room and started to enter. "Ha, you're not going anywhere with your ass hanging out like that!" came her voice from behind the door, and Ethan could only rush to the bathroom and puke in response.

Chapter 3

Ethan was discharged after one more night in the hospital. True to the man in black's word, Dr. Graeme had come moments after he had finished vomiting in the bathroom, but other than the smell, which he couldn't be sure about, he was convinced he'd hidden his stomach ailment pretty well. One thing he was sure of was that he wasn't about to tell anyone about the puking or the man in black. If he did, he knew he'd be stuck here for the foreseeable future, and he wanted out.

It was agreed that his sister would take him home, and the hospital wasn't going to announce Ethan's discharge to anyone in the media. He agreed to a number of future meetings with the airline lawyers, and dodged one person who had snuck in under the guise of being one of them but was actually looking to represent him. "I can get you triple whatever they're offering you! Think about it!" he screamed while being hauled away by hospital security.

Ambulance chasers. Who knew they were actually a thing.

His sister was thankfully low-key when she finally saw him. And after a quick hug, they were guided to an underground parking lot and were instructed how to leave without garnering any suspicion.

He stared out the window and watched as they drove away and toward his apartment without so much as a camera flash. Had some other global distraction deflected the glare of the media away from the only survivor of the "Puget Sound Plunge" (*Christ, why does everything need a catchy name?*)?

"Are you really ok?" Arlene finally asked when they were a few blocks from his place. "I mean really. Don't bullshit me."

He continued to look out the window, hoping to hide whatever lie he was about to tell. "I am. Really. Well, I mean, it's all fucked-up and a plane fell on me and apparently I'm the best thing since Jesus and blowjobs to some people, but yeah, I'll be alright. Thanks for coming, though. I think my car is still in long-term parking at SeaTac."

"I'd take a blowjob from Jesus," she answered. Arlene had always shared his sense of humor, though hers wasn't as black as his had been since she hadn't been around for their mother's really low moments during her final years.

"You'd have to get in line behind those of us with dicks."

The black humor cleared the air a bit and soon they were pulling into his parking lot just outside of downtown. Surprisingly, his car was in his spot, right where it should be.

"Huh. Another gift from the airline, you figure?" Arlene asked.

Ethan shrugged. It likely was. He was their only chance at salvaging anything out of this PR nightmare, so he was easily their favorite person in the world right now. The joke was on them: he was already too emotionally broken and overly-cynical to be won over by these kinds of empty gestures long before they fucked up his life. Still, at least they saved him a trip.

No reporters or revelers were around, likely because Ethan wasn't sure if there was anything that actually tied him to this place as his home. All the bills and utilities were in his roommate's name. He figured it was only a matter of time, though. That kind of information was too easy to get your hands on these days. He'd have to be careful.

They grabbed what little he had to bring in and climbed to the third floor where his loft apartment was. He'd lucked into finding this place after answering an ad he'd seen online before he moved out west. The owner Tony, who was also his roommate, worked at a local Microsoft satellite office and was looking more for a house sitter than a roommate. He was out of town a lot traveling to conferences around the world helping M$ look for another company or technology to buy or put out of business, and he just so happened to take a shine to Ethan and his low-glamour lifestyle. It made sense since anyone could tell when they first met him that Ethan wasn't the "wild parties and weekend booze stupors" kind of guy. He looked like exactly what he was: a young man who just wanted to disappear. Tony never seemed to care from what, and the two rarely spoke even when he was in town, though he had sent flowers and his old Surface tablet to him while he was in the hospital, since Ethan's was likely at the bottom of Puget Sound. Ethan wasn't much to talk to, but he seemed to have earned some kindness somehow.

Once they got in, Ethan was immediately at ease. The cement walls and high ceiling wrapped him up like a blanket. It was stark and industrial, exactly what he was looking for right now. The last ten days had been hell, and he was glad to get back to his Fortress of Solitude.

Just as they were settling in, Arlene couldn't hold back anymore and burst into tears, startling Ethan, who had only just realized that the man in black wasn't here. In fact, he really should have been more cautious when they opened the door. Hadn't he said he would meet him here? Was he even real? God, he hoped this wasn't some Fight Club/Mr. Robot shit.

"Jeez, Arlene, you were doing so well," he said, looking at her as she sat on the couch.

"Fuck you, Ethan. Do you know what this has been like for me? First Mom and then you? Mom I get, but you can't leave me here, too! At least not in the same week!"

"So… I should plan for another week to die? I was the one in a plane crash, you know." He couldn't tell if it was his sarcastic self-defense talking or his genuine need to help his only living relative.

"Just shut up, would you? This isn't the time! I mean, one hundred and thirteen people, Ethan. Gone. One hundred and thirteen funerals being organized right now, and then there's you! How the hell did you live through that?"

He shrugged. How was anyone supposed to answer that question? He figured he'd start with the truth as he knew it. "Soap," he answered honestly.

She sniffled loudly. "What did you just say?"

He sat next to her and slumped back into the well-used but heavenly couch. "Soap. At least, that's what they figured." She continued to look confused. "See, I was near the back of the plane. You know those soap dispensers they have in airplane bathrooms?" Arlene glared like any sane person who'd seen soap before would. "Well, you gotta' fill 'em, right? When the plane ripped apart, the galley at the front of the plane tore open and spilled everything into the water, including a few boxes of soap used to refill those things. Did you know they were called galleys? I just thought they were called plane kitchens. Anyway, when I leapt from the plane, they suspect I hit a pool of the stuff. Just think back to high school science. With how much the plane slowed down as it hit, and the way I jumped, when I hit the water the soap broke the surface tension and I fell into it like hitting a cloud, but, like, at high speed, and I was able to live through it. If I hadn't smacked my head getting out, I likely wouldn't have even needed hospital time, but the concussion made me fall like a ragdoll and hit some shit on the way out. I dunno. Fucked-up, right?"

Her expression was one of bewilderment. "You're shitting me. How the hell do you know that?"

"Some TSA guy who interviewed me told me. He was looking for information about the crash, told me they found me covered in the stuff, that's what they pieced together."

"That's the stupidest thing I've ever heard. Soap?"

"Hey, I agree. I'm not one for miracles, though, so I don't know how much I buy it. But yeah. Fucking soap."

Arlene's face turned red, and for a moment he swore she was going to punch him for lying, even though he actually wasn't (he likely had that same expression when the TSA agent had told him). However, she smiled and just started laughing until she had tears of a different kind rolling down her face.

Ethan couldn't help but join in.

Arlene stayed with him for three more days, but eventually they both had to admit she had to go. She was the executer of their mother's estate (out of stupid luck, since Ethan wasn't legally allowed to be when the will was made), and even for a poor, unwed pill popper, there was still a lot of paperwork to finish.

Ethan made it to a few more meetings, one of which was with a lawyer Tony recommended to represent him who practically gushed with praise when Ethan explained who he was and what he needed. There would be dozens more meetings and other crap he didn't want to go through, but at least this lady would look after the heavy lifting and that meant more people would leave him alone.

Arlene had picked up a new phone for him on one of her outings (he refused an older Windows phone from Tony, because even for free no one wanted one of those), and as soon as he had it reconnected to his number, he instantly regretted it. Although he had time to answer some quick messages and set some things up with people at work, he had one hundred voicemails awaiting him, and that was likely because that was all his system allowed. He wanted to delete them all, but figured some might be from people he actually wanted to speak to, though he doubted it. He'd get to that later. No sooner had he put it down then it started buzzing, showing *The Seattle Times* in the call ID. "No. Thank. You. Off!" and he shut the phone down.

The apartment was silent when Arlene left. Tony, either busy or trying to give the siblings space, hadn't been around much. She hugged him again and looked like she was about to cry. The two had never been extremely close, but the events before the crash led them both to realize that they were all they had left for family. "Are you sure you'll be alright? I feel bad leaving you alone."

"You did it for twenty years. Why stop now?"

"Fuck off, you know what I mean. You haven't been alone yet. It might get freaky. Just don't do anything stupid. I'm only a phone call away."

Ethan had a brief vision of the words the man in black had said about conveniently dying. "Don't worry. I'm way too full of myself to do something crazy. Did you see that there's a small religious movement rising up around my story? I'm a GOD now. Besides, I just messaged some work friends. They'll be here soon. I'll be fine. We're all going to build effigies to other deities and burn them during a crazy ritualistic orgy with me at the center. I've had eyes on the photocopy girl, so she's first. And last too, probably. What can I say; I'm a giver."

"You're a dick, is what you are." She grabbed her wheeler suitcase and headed down the hall. "You're also a miracle. I don't care if you don't believe it. It's not a co-incidence you made it through that."

"I didn't think you believed in miracles, Arlene?"

She smiled back at him, "Just consider that you may be alive for a purpose bigger than… what the hell do you do again?"

"Real estate management company gofer, whipping boy, and general lackey."

"Wow, yeah, I was going to say you're meant for something bigger than that, but by the sounds of it, so is everyone. That sounds horrible."

"Better than nothing. I think I may go back in tomorrow, I love it so much." He didn't, but it didn't offend him, either. It was a ghost job for a ghost man.

"Barely better. Think about it, and don't rush back to work if you don't think you can handle it. Seriously, call me if you need me."

"I will." He wouldn't. "I'll talk to you soon." He also wouldn't. Not unless she called him. Then she was gone, and at long last Ethan was alone.

He puttered around the kitchen for a moment to get a pot of coffee started, eager for a non-shite cup like what the hospital had. Then he went back to the couch and closed his eyes, listening to the sweet sound of nothing of importance.

"Sweet Jésus Christo, I'm glad she's gone. Nice girl, though. How on Earth are you two related?"

Ethan knew that voice instantly. His eyes shot open and he scanned the room. It was getting dark and at first he couldn't see anything, and then the eerie glow of that horrible blonde hairdo materialized out of the kitchen darkness.

He had a black wife-beater tank top on and matching black jeans, with heavy black work boots that clearly didn't match his outfit in anything other than color. His arms were as pale as his face, and he had what looked like a tattoo Ethan couldn't make out on the upper arm below his right shoulder. "I mean, do you have different dads or something?"

Ethan couldn't believe what he was seeing. He quickly looked out the window, remembering their last meeting in the hospital. Unlike that time, cars and pedestrian traffic on the streets still continued.

"Relax, kid. It's why I waited until we were finally alone. I hate messing with the fabric of time if I can avoid it. It just creates more work when I'm done. Or when you're done, if you catch my meaning."

"I don't. How the hell did you get in here?"

"No, of course you don't. And to answer that second part, I'd guess you'd have to use your non-existent imagination, because whatever I tell you about how I got here isn't going to sound real, so you may as well just make something up."

"You're imaginary and I'm freaking the fuck out."

29

"Wow… you came up with something faster than I expected. No, Ethan, I'm not imaginary. I'm as real as real gets. Realer, even. I kinda go beyond real some days. It's part of the job."

"What job?"

"Here we go again… Death, stupid. It's a job. It's a name. It's a state of being!" He was animated, but still composed, talking with his hands and step-gliding towards where Ethan was still sitting. He ended up taking a seat opposite Ethan, leaning forward like a man looking to continue to engage in this conversation.

"You're in my head. You have to be. This shit can't be real."

"No, I've said, it is real. Realer than real. I'm Death. Trust me, it doesn't get any realer than me."

"Why… why are you here?"

The man clapped his hands, a loud sound that echoed through the studio apartment sharply. "At last, a non-stupid question, and a good one too. Well, Ethan, I'm here to offer you a job. My job. And by offer, I mean force it upon you in ways you may not like. I guess I could say I'm here to job-rape you, but that seems a bit crass."

"Thanks, but no thanks. Your pyramid scheme sales pitch fucking sucks."

"You don't seem to be listening. This isn't about peddling Amway or finding out what's behind door number two. It's this, or it's this, but a little bit later than I'd like because you're being an ass about this and dragging it out. Either way, it's happening."

"What if I don't want your job, because spoiler alert: I fucking don't."

He looked away, rolling his eyes so hard Ethan thought he could hear them. "God I hate that term… Look, do I have to go back to the job-rape analogy, because I will, kid. It's rude, but I will." The man claiming to be Death stood again and wandered into the kitchen. Without hitting a switch, the fluorescents above him turned on, causing Ethan to squint at the harsh new light. "I was pissed at you, Ethan. You have no idea how angry I was. Hell, I still am, but I'm keeping a lid on it."

"Pissed about what? Living through a plane crash?"

"Yes, God damn it!" the man whirled and his eyes almost burned a hole through Ethan with their intensity. It was the same jittery look he had in the hospital hallway. "It was a fucking plane crash! You don't *live* through that kind of thing. You die! You die tragically! You die and others die and everyone dies and they build some cheap monument in your honor on the shore near where it happened and then decades from now when no one remembers why it's there anymore some asshole developer buys the land that monument is on and has it moved into storage where it gets shit on by rats for all eternity while he builds condos that he sells at disgusting prices! That's what you do when you're a part of a national tragedy!"

Ethan had no answer. The man was giving voice to the same thoughts Ethan had had over the last week.

"But, *but*, I'm not *as* angry now. I had a few drinks, ferried a few souls, and ate something called muhammara on a business trip to Syria for that ongoing genocide that is happening and is horrible and nobody anywhere cares anything about, and now I'm coming at this task with a new point of view. I just needed you alone before I could talk to you about it. Is that coffee I smell?"

"Can Death smell things?"

"Death can smell coffee. That's it though. May I?"

Still shocked at the intrusion, but unsure what else he should be doing in this situation, Ethan indicated he help himself. Besides, it kept him across the room, as far away in the apartment as he could get without actually leaving.

Death rattled around the kitchen until he found the mugs and poured himself a cup. "Cream and sugar?"

Dumbfounded, Ethan started to stammer that the sugar was in the little pantry in the corner when Death cut him off. "I'm just kidding. Obviously I take it black. This isn't Starbucks is it? Heaven help you if it's Starbucks."

"It's not," Ethan answered. "Tony used to work for them. He said they were too evil to support and he left. I just think it tastes like burnt shit."

"You're both right," Death answered, taking a sip. He gave the standard *meh, not bad* eyebrow twitch and sat back down. "So, back to business. I have a proposition for you, since obviously going the traditional route isn't going to work. So let's talk about it briefly, and then you go get some sleep in that travesty of a bed I know you've been missing, and tomorrow you and I will go on a wonderful tour of all existence while I describe how I'm going to force my vaunted position of Charon on to you. Do you have school tomorrow?"

"I work."

"Can you call in sick?"

"No."

"Can you call in dead?"

"Um… No? At least I doubt it. I've never tried. Am I going to be dead?"

"Only if I do my job right. And by that I mean be convincing enough to make you do what I want you to do, not, like, actually doing my job, although I guess that would apply here too."

Ethan just gawked at him while he continued to drink the coffee. They sat in silence staring at each other, with Ethan trying to judge the reality of the situation, when there was a knock on the door which startled them both. "Ugh, never a moment's peace. You know, for a loner you sure don't seem very lonely." Death stood and slammed back what was left of the coffee, even though it still had to be scorching. "Alright, get some sleep. I'll see you tomorrow. Big day! Cosmic balance. Mysteries of the universe. Your noble, tragic death. My well-earned retirement. Oh yes, quite a day ahead."

With that, he set the coffee down on the counter by the sink and disappeared, just like in the hospital. Only the mug remained to prove he was even there in the first place.

Chapter 4

The rest of the night was just a blur, as Ethan let his friends in and listened to them prattle on about how lucky he is, how sorry they were that he had to go through it, reaffirming the sorrow about his mother, blah blah blah. Amy the photocopy girl even cried a few times from being so overwhelmed by Ethan's ten days from Hell. Maybe an orgy wasn't out of the question?

They poured a bunch of beers and carried on about nothing in particular after the novelty of sharing an evening with a living Lazarus wore off. Ethan had only been in Seattle for ten months, so no one here was really what he'd call close, but an oddly sentimental part of him did appreciate the company. Although he was never much of a drinker (*thanks again, Mom*) by the end of the night he was drunk and the Man Who Would Be Death was just a blurry memory.

His friends shuffled out around 2am, and he wasn't sure but he could have sworn Amy's hands lingered on his back a little longer and more sensuously than he expected. Once she kissed him on the cheek and told him to call her if he needed anything, he was a hair's-width away from asking her to stay, but the leering eyes of his three other friends in the doorway immediately embarrassed him out of the thought. Fuck you, social anxiety.

"Are you going to be at work soon? Or does that fat settlement I'm sure you're due mean we've seen the last of you?" she asked.

"Yeah, actually I was thinking about coming in tomorrow. Better than sitting around here. Besides, the settlement is a long time out. Still gotta eat."

"You know, we were thinking about setting up a Go-FundMe page for you, if you wanted. I'll bet half the country would…"

Even drunk, Ethan's anxious stomach tightened and he waved her off. The others tried to insist as well, but he was adamant. "No, no way. No charity. No strangers pouring sappy well-wishes down my throat like jizz. From what I've heard, the airline will give more than enough, even after taxes and fees and people swindling me out of most of it. I'm good. Seriously, I want to work." He didn't. He was going to quit just as soon as the settlement came in. He had no idea what he was going to do then, but Arlene was right: anything was better than what he was doing, now that he had the money to do it.

"Well, no rush mate," said Chris, his Australian boss and generally good guy, as near as he could tell. "In your own time. I can get my own coffee, at least for a few days." He smiled at his own joke and led the group away.

Once the door closed Ethan made a half-hearted look around to see if Death would pop up again like he had when Arlene left, but the place was silent. The mug, however, remained on the counter.

Death Dresses Poorly

Ethan had never set an alarm in his life. He was blessed with a body clock that would wake him up as and when he needed it, be it for school, work, or his mother's hospital visits. Even after a late night of drinking, his eyes opened at a quarter to eight, as if his body was telling him to go to work, even if his head protested.

Once he was awake, the coffee smell hit him. He never set his coffee maker to go on automatically because he got free coffee at work. He didn't think Tony would be home, but he supposed it was possible.

Then the haze cleared, and he remembered what Death had said. He instantly started to panic.

"I know you're up now, kid. Might as well c'mon out!" Yep. It was Death. How did he know Ethan was awake?

He closed his eyes and slowly slipped under the sheets, waiting to see if it was a dream. Almost at once a hand gripped the bedspread and pulled, yanking the sheets off completely and hitting Ethan with a rush of cold air as he lay there in just his boxers. "Look, seriously, let's get going. Quit spanking it to the little blonde photocopy girl and come join me. It's a busy day!" And again he disappeared like a ghost. Seeing as he was now sheet-less and cold, Ethan had to assume it wasn't a dream. He sat up slowly, grabbed a shirt and a pair of warm-up pants from the chair next to his bed, threw on his glasses, and stepped out into the loft.

Death sat at the little kitchen table, mug in hand, looking over a newspaper that appeared to be in a language Ethan couldn't understand. He wore black board shorts that didn't suit a man of his age (did he have an age?) and his black turtleneck. On his feet was a pair of matching black Crocs. He was no longer wearing glasses.

"Wakey wakey, sunshine. The day is new, and so is my attitude! C'mon. Grab a cup. I brought you a treat."

Still unsure, Ethan stepped to the coffeemaker as Death indicated and looked at the black bag next to it. It was a brand of coffee he'd never seen before. "I brought it back just for you. It's from Canada! Crazy, eh? You'd figure the best coffee in the world would be Columbian or Hawaiian or that stuff that's shit out of a cat in Sumatra, but nope. It's from some hidden town in the Canadian Rockies. Good'ol Canadians. Boring as shit, though." Ethan wasn't sure he knew any Canadians. "Go on, pour yourself a cup and join me."

"I don't drink coffee at home usually. I get it at work for free."

"Hey, I said this was a gift, so it's as free as free can be. No strings attached. And since you're not going to work today, I guess you lucked out that I made this for you."

"Why aren't I going to work again?" Ethan wanted to make sure that what Death had told him the night before was true and not just a creation of the booze or mild hangover.

"Because today is the day I teach you about your brand-new job. I take you around, show you the sights, pass on the title, and by dinner you'll be begging me to just retire already and let you get started. Or, you could try to go back to your fulfilling job of being a wage slave with no future. You won't, though." The man claiming to be Death straightened his back and sharply pulled his shirt down to imitate wearing a crisp suit instead of a bland, out of place turtleneck. "I'm too charming to lose this fight."

Ethan could only scoff at the bravado. "Oh, clearly." He sat silently for a moment, seeming to ponder what was being said. "Being dead sure doesn't sound like it has a lot of room for growth, to be honest. Maybe I'm missing something, but I can't see a lot of possible upward mobility."

"Oh don't be so sure. You've never been dead before. Care to try it out before we get started?" From thin air, Death pulled out the largest handgun Ethan had ever seen and set it on the table. "Go on, let's get right to it. Just a little click click, bang bang, and my job will be all but done."

Ethan just stared at the weapon in horror. Even growing up in Chicago, he'd never had much taste for guns. "Oh, relax," Death assured, pawing in the air towards Ethan like a cat chasing a toy. "I've got a permit to carry. It's right here..." He searched the cargo pockets in his board shorts, but came out emptyhanded. "Well, I had one. Don't tell the feds!" and just as it arrived, the weapon vanished. Death settled back into his chair again. "Look, pour a coffee and sit down. It's de-lic-ious."

Ethan decided to see how this fever dream played out, but he always kept his mind on the fact that it wasn't real, and something fucked his head up after the funeral and the plane crash. He grabbed his favorite mug and poured a fresh cup. It sure did smell good.

Never taking his eyes off of the man at the table, Ethan walked over and sat opposite him. He had a small sip of the coffee and was surprised to find that although he usually didn't have much taste for what was good or bad in the coffee world, this tasted pretty good.

"I told you so." Death smiled at him. "No one knows a decent coffee better than the Grim Reaper. Count on it. So, let's discuss our day, shall we?"

"I told you, I'm going to work," Ethan answered.

"Hmm, you sure about that?" Death asked back.

Ethan raised his eyebrows mockingly. "Hmm. I could go to work, or I could hang out all day with a guy who says he's Death. Tough call. Probably work…" He took another sip. Still delicious.

"Ok, I admit I've come off as a bit aggressive, but you need to know that you've put me in a bit of a predicament here. People don't just live through plane crashes. It's not natural. Your will to live is like nothing I've ever encountered. What's it like not being natural?"

"Yep, that's me. Unnatural as the day is long. What can I say, I'm just a stickler for the classics, like Zeppelin and *Seinfeld* and living."

Death put the mug he was holding down hard on the table, spilling more than a small amount over the side. He looked at the mess angrily, his eyes starting their familiar twitch. Ethan watched as Death seemed to cool himself before he proceeded. "Look, kid. This is all fun and games to you, but there's something coming. Something big.

Universe-changing big, and unless you hadn't noticed, the universe is the place where you live. I need you for it. I need you and only you. Trust me, if a regular Deathmore would do, I'd have found one by now."

"A what?"

"A Deathmore. Something in the infinite cosmos that has what it takes to be Death, because this gig isn't permanent. We get in, we do our job, and we retire peacefully when we're done. Take me for example. I was a Deathmore. I was recruited because of you. My whole role was chosen because of all the creatures available in the universe, I was the best one for the job of recruiting you. Pretty sad, huh?"

"Yep. I'd kinda hoped famous fictional deities would be better at their jobs."

"Ha, have you ever read Greek mythology? Those assholes are nothing if not unreliable dickheads." Ethan had, but he didn't remember much about them other than what Liam Neeson had taught him. Something about Krackens…

Death looked at Ethan thoughtfully. "Look kid, like I said, I'm coming at this from a fresh angle. Maybe it's the ability to see this angle that had me recruited in the first place. Who knows. I'm not the boss."

"Who's the boss?"

"Well I always thought it was Tony Danza, but a case could be made for Mona…"

Ethan started to get angry now. He hated getting jerked around. "Look, ass, you know what I mean. You want to talk, so let's talk. Who's your boss? Who do you answer to? God?"

"God is such a vague term…"

"I'd say it's pretty damn clear."

"Is it? Is it clear? Your God? No, you don't strike me as a 'God' type, but yours as in the generic WASP Christian God? Allah? Odin? The duck the crazy homeless guy down the street worships? Looks like that answer is a little complicated."

"Fine, then tell me who you answer to. Enlighten me."

"Jeez, I don't have that kind of time. I just want to convince you to take my job. Enlightenment of a sarcastic twenty-year-old jerk is out of my paygrade."

Ethan grabbed his mug and turned to go back to his room. "Fine, fuck off then. I have a job to get ready for. Any idea what I should wear to work?"

Death shrugged. "Irrelevant. You won't survive the day."

"So, no tie then?"

Ethan heard Death sigh audibly as he entered his room. He wasn't turning out to be much of a cosmic entity, if that's indeed what he was. Ethan still wasn't convinced, although every aspect of his senses told him this was really happening and wasn't in his head. The coffee was too good for him to assume he'd made it himself in his own mind. Death had been right: he didn't have much of an imagination. He decided to keep digging deeper.

"Look, I don't want to tell you how to do your job or anything, but if you're actually Death, shouldn't you be off in the world collecting souls or hanging out invisibly next to some old lady who's about to have a heart attack or something?"

"Who's to say I'm not? You have no idea how many living things die every second. If you'd just come along and listen to me, I know I could get you to understand. Death isn't just a single thing. It's a concept. It's a universal tool of energetic dispersal. I'm just an attractive voice for something so much larger."

"Like the Borg Queen on Star Trek?"

"Yes, Ethan. Just like the Borg Queen on Star Trek. What an apt analogy. Why didn't I think of it? It's so clear to me now. I just needed to describe my infinitely important galactic responsibility as being like robots from a show that went off the air twenty years ago. How stupid I am to not make that connection."

"Hey, you said it, man. I'm just trying to piece it together."

"I thought you were getting ready for work."

"I can do more than one thing at a time. Shocking, I know."

"No you can't. You're a man. You have precision focus on just one thing at a time. How fast you can change that focus is what determines your course of action."

"And what are you?"

"Not a man."

"Sorry, what *were* you?"

"A squirrel. A girl one at that."

Ethan stopped and looked back out the door. "A what?"

"A squirrel. A girl squirrel. Sciuridae Femella. Did I stutter?"

Ethan wasn't sure how to answer this new piece of information, but a part of him realized it could explain the constant twitchiness when Death was agitated. "I... uh... Really? Like, those little buggers that steal all the bird seed?"

"Congratulations. You know what a squirrel is. Yes. That was me. Happy little squirrel. Happy little squirrel life. Burying nuts for winter. Having numerous broods of little squirrel babies after crazy squirrel sex."

"Why would a squirrel be the best choice to recruit me in all the world?"

"World? You think too small. We're talking all the universes here, man. Infinite cosmos. It all came down to me. And yet here we are. What a joke."

"Where?"

Death looked at him with an eyebrow raised. "Where what?"

"Where were you a squirrel? Like, in Central Park or Namibia or something? What kind of squirrel were you? How..."

Death raised his hands in mock defense. "Whoa, whoa, easy there Mr. Curious. One question at a time, and only when I choose to answer. There's too much else to do to be wrapped up in our honeymoon phase."

"Fine, I get that, since you seem to be in such a rush, but help me out here Squirrel Girl."

Death looked at Ethan with a gaze that could melt lead even from this far across the room. He clearly didn't like being mocked about his rodent origins. Ethan was taken aback by the ferocity of it, but didn't back down. By his own admission, Death couldn't kill him.

However, he may be able to hurt him really badly.

Wait a minute... Was Ethan admitting to himself that this thing might actually be Death, and for that matter, could be trusted? What was even more troubling was that he almost wanted to believe Death. Would being Death really be so bad? It could be an interesting change of pace if nothing else.

He wasn't sure why, but something told him, deep in places he rarely listened to, that he was what he said he was. Or, she was? God, this was too much for this time in the morning.

Death relaxed. "Look, let's take a step back here. Too much exposition upfront can make a great story terrible. Let's leave the smartass remarks and squirrel comments to ourselves, ok? Let's enjoy this beautiful Canadian coffee over here, and I'll try a bit harder to not break my galactic mandate not to murder you horribly."

Ethan pulled on a shirt that didn't offend him when he smelled it, but stopped short of finishing getting ready for work. "That'll be pretty hard. I'm easy to want to kill."

"Tell me about it."

A calm silence passed between them, and Ethan finished getting ready. He wasn't really dressed for work, but he wasn't really in grubs either. He was his usual ghostly medium, just like he was with everything in life.

"Alright, clearly human male, let's start fresh. You're really Death?"

"Yes. Really."

"And you want to hire me to take your job?"

"*Hire* makes it sound like you have a choice, or a chance to not take it, but sure."

"And if I go with you now, you won't murder me in some elaborate trap with a bunch of rapists and shit in the back of some sketchy van when we get outside?"

"Hmm, interesting vision. What's on the side of the van in this horror story?"

"Nothing. It's a mom van. Airbrushed panel vans are more child-molester than murdering rapist."

"Strange thing for a guy to know."

"Look, you're saying you're on the level or not?"

"Level as a plumb line. You bet."

"But if I make it to the end of your crazy acid trip, I want to know I can say *no*, and if I do I get to go back to my normal life, and you'll leave me alone."

Death shuddered. Similar deals to this always had bad consequences. "I intended to show you so many things which will confuse and amaze you that you'll never be normal again."

They both caught the fact that it wasn't a yes or no, but Ethan let it slide. He wasn't going to win a war of words with Death. If anyone knew the tricks, it would be him.

Ethan pulled on some jeans, placed his glasses in their cloth case which he then put in his pocket, and came back over to the table to finish his delicious coffee. "This is a seriously fucked-up week."

Death folded and put down his paper. "My young apprentice, you don't know the half of it." Death rose up and headed for the door, kitchen light blinking out behind him as he moved leaving Ethan in the dark as his Crocs clopped across the hardwood.

Ethan grabbed a coat and sneakers and followed after the black entity with the bad sun-bleached hair in front of him.

"Do you want to grab a bite to eat first?" Death asked as they entered the hallway, closing the door behind them.

"Fine, but you're buying."

"Death doesn't carry cash."

"How fucking convenient."

Chapter 5

The man in the terrible black attire stepped from the building, followed by the skeptical face of the survivor of the *Puget Plunge (*Copyright pending.) The sky was cloudy now, and the winter chill was strong as the mist blew around.

"Jesus, doesn't this city have any weather other than rain or fog?"

"We have drizzle. This is really more of a drizzle."

"Ugh. Fucking Seattle. Whatever. Let's go this way. I know a place."

Ethan followed after the sure strides of the tall man. He was pretty sure he knew every breakfast joint in this part of the city by now, not being a man who enjoyed cooking for himself, and he was certain none of them were in this particular direction.

They walked in silence for a time, but eventually Ethan was too curious to keep it that way. This situation needed to be reckoned. "Ok, so is this supposed to be like 'A Christmas Carole' or something? And you're here to teach me a lesson and reflect on my life or some shit like that?"

Death kept looking forward as he walked, his board shorts slowly starting to drip as they got wetter in the rain. "Ugh. That sounds horrible. You're too boring. I've seen your life, Ethan Dessier, and your life is about as white-bread as it gets."

"My mother may have disagreed with you."

"Please, your mother was the only thing that gave you a shred of being anything interesting, and instead of embracing that, you ran half-way across the country to escape it and let her die alone."

Ethan stopped instantly, eyes burning into the back of Death's sun-bleached head. "Fuck this bullshit, ass. I have better things to do with my time than get guilt-tripped by you."

"Ha. We both know that's not true. That's the whole point of this conversation." Death turned and looked at Ethan clearly. If the cold and rain was getting to him at all, he showed zero sign of it. "Look, kid; like I said in Chicago, I'm sorry about that… but not really, right? Even for me, it's just a thing we say. I'm not out to wound you emotionally, and don't give me this noble crap like I'm telling you something you don't want to hear and don't already know. It's too 'fifteen-year-old-girl' of you. You left your mom and you believe it was the right thing to do. You couldn't save her, and she was only sinking your ship, right?" No answer. Just continued glowering. "So, yeah, you ran away, and not many in your place could have done better. You're here getting on with your life and actually trying to salvage what's left of it while she's worm food. I may not agree, but I *get* it."

"Do you think I was wrong?"

Death looked down for a moment, as if trying to choose the right words, but then looked up and shrugged.

"I know you were. That's not fair, though, because I see things you can't."

Ethan went from angry red to sickly white in an instant. Had Death just told him his mother's death was preventable if he'd only stayed?

Before he could come to grips with the possibility, Death interjected, "But I'll tell you this, and I mean this since lying isn't something I'm wholly capable of: you didn't make her death worse by not being there. By the end, it was what she wanted. She sought release and it was finally granted. She knew it was coming and she made her peace with it, or at least the dying part of it. She was still scared to death (job humor) about what came after, but she worked it out. And I'll tell you something else, whether you want to hear it or not: you and your sister weren't even a blip on her mental radar when she left this world. She never cared enough or was lucid enough to fully grasp what being a mother really was."

Death was clearly trying his best not to set off the emotional bomb building inside Ethan. "Now, I'm saying this not to piss you off or throw you into another hissy tantrum, but to confirm what you already suspected: your mom was a shit mom who did shit things to herself and those around her, but in the end she died peacefully and your presence or absence didn't change anything *to her*. Now that I have laid all of that out for you, let it sink in, and come get some waffles with me."

Ethan stood in the drizzle, slowly getting colder and colder now that he wasn't moving. He loved his mom, in a strange, mentally abused and obligatory sort of way.

There had been good times. Maybe even great ones, if he thought about it, but Death only confirmed what he suspected all along, and that was that without him and his sister, she ended up the same way. Maybe what Death meant before was that she would have lived if he stayed, but it wouldn't have been a good life. Something to talk about later, he supposed.

Death turned and slowly started walking away, and after a moment of horrible self-reflection, Ethan followed. Waffles were suddenly the most important thing in the world to him, and he was damned if he was going to miss out on them.

The two walked on. Ethan held his coat tight against his body to fight the February chill, but Death simply walked confidently, his ridiculous Crocs clomping along like Dutch clogs on the cold sidewalk. "I hate to tell you this, but there are no restaurants this way. It's just uppity shoe stores and pot shacks."

"Ah Washington. A state after my own heart. All the natural majesty in the world to offer, and a populace too in love with itself to notice it unless they're so high they think it's a trip." Ethan had to agree to that. He never touched drugs as a rule, and unlike most addict kids, he found it a pretty easy one to follow. "Trust me, kid. When I know a place, I'm not usually wrong about its existence."

They carried on a few more blocks and stopped outside a corner convenience store that looked like it had seen better days. Death looked up at the logo above the door that proclaimed the cheapest rolling papers in town and took a large whiff. "Ahhh, smell those pastries. I'm telling you, you're in for a treat. And I mean that literally. Like, doughnuts and croissants and shit, if you want."

Ethan looked up confused, but there was nothing in the air but cold, wet earth and something organically putrid wafting from the building. "This better be a joke, because I'm hungry as hell and I'm getting late for work. There's nothing here but a shitty store."

"I'll thank you not to talk about this place so crudely. The owner is particularly uppity about people besmirching her establishment."

Ethan rolled his eyes and looked back down the street where they'd come from, mentally calculating if he could run back and start off for work in time to catch the early-morning free muffins usually on offer. The road was hazy, and the cars seemed to drift through it as if they were driving into or out of a choppy ocean. The whole place was being eaten by a fog rolling in off the Sound now to top off the ethereal feeling.

"You coming in or what?" Death called from behind him as he stepped up the single stair to the entrance door and opened it.

Ethan spun back around and was about to rip Death a new one yet again when he noticed something was very different. The dilapidated vinyl exterior of the store was now a pristine tan brick, and any hints of its run-down nature were gone, replaced with what looked like a picturesque breakfast diner. The sign above the door now read: "Crystal's Café. Come on in for the best waffles in town!"

Ethan stepped back, shocked. He almost stepped off the curb and into oncoming traffic, but caught himself just before a red car from a brand he'd never seen before (*"Holden"*?) whizzed past, blasting its horn as it went.

Death snapped his fingers in disappointment, commanding Ethan's attention again. "Damn it. So close. Here I thought a lot of needless talk was going to be avoided. But, I guess if a fucking airplane won't kill you, a Holden Commodore would bounce off you like a flea. C'mon. We're letting the outside in, and Crystal will get pissed."

Startled and confused, Ethan crawled up the lone step and came to his feet, quickly stepping inside. He found himself in a pleasant-smelling diner, typical of many he'd been to, which would be great if he wasn't positive that it was a shitty corner store made for potheads only a few moments before.

Death led him in and sat him at a booth by the window. Despite the time of day, it was strangely vacant, with only a few others sitting around dining silently.

"You want to tell me what the fuck that was?" Ethan asked incredulously, looking around like he'd just been released from a solitary confinement cell and put straight into Disneyland.

"It was a Holden Commodore. Pretty average mid-sized Australian sedan, and common as flies around here." Ethan stopped and looked at him, clearly giving off the impression that the mysterious car wasn't what he was referring to. "Oh, you mean the restaurant. I'm sorry, did you assume your reality was the only one? I just picked one with better waffles nearby is all. I'd say you could thank me, but since you're still paying regardless of what world we're in, I'll let it slide. Shit… I hope your money is still good here. Is Washington or Clinton on the twenty?"

"Clin… Clinton?" Ethan asked, as if trying to make sense of his own words.

"Yes, Clinton. George Clinton. Founding Father? Vice President and then longest serving President in the history of these United States? At least he was in most realities. You know what, it doesn't matter. Just pass it off fast and no one will notice." Death picked up a menu and started reading.

Ethan stopped and stared at the back of Death's menu, as if the look itself were words enough to demand an answer. "Why was there an Australian car on Seattle streets? What kind of fucked-up magic was being used to change the look of the diner?"

He was about to start screaming for answers when an incredibly pretty young waitress came over with a notepad and a hot pot of coffee, which she instinctively poured out into their cups before setting it aside and preparing herself to take their order. Before he could say anything, she looked at him with round brown eyes and started speaking a language that was unlike anything Ethan had ever heard before. It was mostly clicks and tongue rolls.

He could only stare at her confused when Death started responding in the same strange way, as if he was just carrying on another conversation. She looked at him, seemed to ask a question or two back (according to her body language, anyway) and the two carried on like that for a moment. Ethan could only watch the attractive woman and Death in confusion.

"Waffles, yeah? You were serious?" Death asked suddenly, pulling his dining partner out of his baffled stupor. "You don't want them in some fu-fu whole wheat, extra flax, hold the syrup way, do you?"

Ethan started to come around. "What? What? No… No, just regular please. Fuck flax."

"Ha, God damned right! Fuck flax in its fat flax ass!" Death smiled back at him while Ethan looked embarrassed at the waitress. "Oh cool your love rockets, sexy boy. This glorious pancake-house angel can't understand a word we're saying." With that, Death looked back at the girl, nodded while saying something incoherent, and handed her his menu. She took it and looked at Ethan expectantly. Eventually he clued in and passed his back as well, and she left to place the order, but not before passing a sly wink at Ethan as she left.

Death smirked while he sipped his coffee, catching the flirtatiousness at once. "Oooo, see what being exotic gets you? In some places all you need is a foreign language to get a bit of tail."

"I'm not foreign. I'm from six blocks away!" Ethan cried, getting angrier at the situation as it grew stranger.

"Look kid, right here, in this place, in this world, you're about as out of town as it gets. Get used to it."

"In this world? You brought me to another world? Like, a different dimension and shit?" Ethan looked around again in a quasi-panic, trying to find anything else that may have been out of place. As near as he could tell, it was still just a diner. The few people he could see were just doing diner things like reading papers, chatting quietly, or ringing through a check at the till. Nothing suggested other-dimensional travel in the in-your-face way the movies said it would.

"Of course I did. Your reality's waffles suck! And if you use another *Star Trek* analogy, so help me God…"

"What the hell, man!" Ethan shouted, gathering looks from around the sparsely-populated room. "You don't just drop trans-dimensional travel on a guy! I mean, a little warning or something would have been nice!"

Death raised his blonde eyebrow at Ethan, amused. "Warning? Like, an alarm or something? Or a quick punch in the arm while I say, 'Hang on kid, we're going to a place where people shit out of their fingertips!' because that's a thing I've seen, and don't think it's not. Oh Christ… I hope that's not here…" He quickly looked around, panicked. "Thank God. It's not. The trees here are green."

Ethan stared at Death dumbfounded. After funerals and plane crashes and all kinds of craziness, Ethan was pretty sure this was it. He was gone. Lost into a world of madness. He was likely floating face-down in a bathtub somewhere and this was just an elaborate dream his brain conjured up to make his passing more painful and confusing, since he just knew that was how it was going to go when he died. Nothing was ever easy.

"Look, eat your waffles. Drink a cup of sub-standard coffee, and just listen to what I have to say. This place is step one: thinking outside the box, and your whole existence is effectively *the box*."

Now that his eyes were a bit more open, Ethan began noticing things he'd missed. The signs were still all in perfectly legible English, but the quiet conversations he could hear were in the same off clicks and sounds the waitress had made. In the far corner, a man was drinking what looked a lot like bright green milk. A song was playing from the kitchen and it was a tune he recognized, but it seemed off, like notes were playing in the wrong place or in a slightly different key.

"Why can I read the signs?" Ethan asked as Death quietly sipped his coffee and let him figure things out on his own. "If the language is different, why can I still see English?"

"Who says English can only be pronounced one way? Subtle changes in history can make a lot of things different, while also being the same. There's a whole legion of universes that use base-eight math as the norm. Do you know how confusing that is? Leaving a tip is an exercise in quantum mechanics."

Soon the waitress returned and set down two identical plates of waffles with a side of home fries and a mix of fruit that included something blue Ethan didn't recognize. With a smile and a few humming clicks, she was gone. Ethan looked at the meal.

"What's the blue stuff?"

"Caddles."

"What the fuck is a caddle?"

"Those blue things. Weren't you paying attention? This isn't your home. This isn't where you're from. I picked a place just far enough left of center that you won't freak out, but would at least start your listening skills. I could have gone full-asshole and taken you straight to the place where everything is upside-down and pink or perceived through a fifth-dimensional lens." Death bit into his waffles, and tossed a couple of caddles in when he was done. "C'mon, live a little. It's a fruit no one from your neck of the woods has ever seen or heard of before. You're a pioneer in fruit testing!"

Skeptical, Ethan stuck a fork into the blue crunchy fruit and took a bite. Instantly his mouth was assaulted with an acrid and charred flavor, as if he'd bitten a leftover piece of burned firewood. He spit it out at once, trying to pry the remnants of it off his tongue. He lunged for the coffee and let its thankfully familiar flavor wash the taste away. "You dick! That was disgusting! I feel like I just bit a nightclub ashtray!"

Death looked at Ethan confused, and then simply shrugged. "Huh. You might not like the waffles, then."

"What about the strawberry?"

"Try it and see."

Ethan did. Although not offensive like the caddle was, it still didn't taste that great, and it certainly didn't taste anything like a strawberry. Ethan sniffed the waffle. It smelled like fresh pipe tobacco. Pass. He ate the rest of his fruit that didn't offend him, for no other reason than to get something into his stomach, and finished his coffee.

Death cleaned his plate, caddles and all, and called the waitress over. After indicating Ethan's plate and pointing to his own stomach while talking in the non-English English to her, she smiled and turned slightly red, and then cleared their plates.

Ethan caught on immediately. "You told her I had fucking diarrhea or some shit, didn't you?"

Death looked momentarily shocked and then started laughing. It was a deep laugh, as if it came from a place so far down in his body that it was almost unfathomable. "Not bad," he said when he was finished. "You're God-damned right I did. With blood in it and everything."

"What the fuck, man!" Ethan screamed, turning red himself. His social anxiety coupled with good old-fashioned embarrassment flushed him as deep a shade as a tomato as he looked toward the back to see if she was laughing at him. Other dimensions or not, pretty girls were pretty girls.

"Oh relax," Death replied, still grinning. "It won't matter in seventeen seconds anyway."

Ethan stopped looking for the girl and sat again. "What do you mean?"

"I mean, in fifteen seconds, the blissful — and dare I say sexual — image she has in her head right now of nursing the exotic, brooding lad in booth six back to health will be the last thing on her mind. Literally."

Before he could fully realize what Death meant, a male voice from out back screamed in the unintelligible language, drawing Ethan's attention. "What did he say?" Ethan began to ask, before he was cut off by a massive fireball enveloping the kitchen with a *whoosh* speeding outwards, quickly consuming the diners seated closest to the source.

Ethan panicked and dove backwards behind a wall of cabinets that held the trash can while the fireball kept pouring out, blowing out some windows and smashing plates as it moved. Soon, there was nothing but the roar of the explosion, and Ethan covered his ears and squinted against the brightness.

And then, there was only silence.

…which was suddenly broken by that same guttural laugh. "He said, 'Run! I hit a gas line!' obviously. Wow, do you look stupid. Nice dive, though. Very MacGuyver-esque. Pick your ass up. We have work to do."

Chapter 6

The scene was completely surreal. Ethan stood from his cowering position behind the trash cabinets and tried to let his brain process what he was seeing.

Death had begun to step towards the wall of fire, which was now frozen in time and silent. He moved slowly, surveying the scene, almost seeming to make mental notes. Eventually he paused and looked back at the wide-eyed Ethan. "C'mon. Seriously, it's a major pain to freeze time like this. The universe tends to protest after a while, so just roll with me, okay? The fire won't hurt you. I've removed us from time to show you the next part of this glorious job offer."

Ethan could admit that he didn't find any heat coming from the fire in front of him, so he slowly worked his way out to where Death was standing. He reached his hand out to where the first licks of flame were stretching forward. He felt nothing. "Crazy, right?" said Death watching him. "It's just a split second in time, but it tells such a story. A tragic one, too. Follow me, please."

The black-clad Death stepped into the fire unflinchingly, working his way towards the kitchen entrance where the pretty young server was before the flames consumed her. Tentative at first, Ethan followed, testing the fire before fully committing and tracing Death's steps.

He was just ahead, standing next to a shadow Ethan couldn't make out. When he got closer, his stomach turned when he realized it was the darkened, burned husk of the girl he'd had flirting with him just moments before. Her clothes were on fire and charred almost to the point of indecency. Her hair was all but gone, leaving only a scorched head. She had been frozen in place while falling backwards, her blackened arms held up in front of her burning face as she let out a scream. The fire all around the three added to the washed-out bizarreness of the scene.

"This," Death indicated the girl, "is Omally. No, I'll stop you there, it's not a weird name. Omally is a pretty common name in this place. Like Karen or Jen or Zebby. Anyway, she is just working as a server to earn some cash to move to California."

"Let me guess," Ethan piped in, trying to distract himself from the burning girl who threatened to bring back up the fruit and coffee he'd just put down, "Hollywood bound? Gonna' be a star and all that?"

Death looked at him as if he had just spoken a language he didn't recognize. "Huh? What? No, no she wants to move to the Bay Area and work towards being a marine biologist. The weather is just better there than it is here. Is everything a cliché to you?" Ethan looked away embarrassed. "Anyway, I can tell you this about her: she's a strong one. Or at least, she was. Raised by a single Dad who passed away a few years ago. Nice personality. Good friends who will miss her. She was all of the best things about people, for no reason at all other than that she chose to be."

"Are you saying I'm not strong?" Ethan asked, defensively. "That I could have been her somehow?"

Death looked about ready to say something snarky back, but then turned his eyes down. "No. Your predilection for being a sourpuss is in your DNA. Some things people simply can't change about themselves. Some caveman deep in your genealogy had some other Neanderthal shit in his nuts and berries and your line has been a downer ever since. But this one, she was cheery as the summer sun. I know she's strong, because this is her first and only time doing this."

Ethan looked from the floating body and back to Death. "Doing what?"

"Dying, clearly," Death replied. "This one has never died before and won't again. She had one crack at this, and she just used it. That's how I know she's strong. She saw a giant flaming wall of death and right here, in this moment, she is accepting her death. She doesn't feel cheated. She doesn't feel sad. She has no regrets. She knows it is what it needs to be, so she has embraced the moment and is ready to go." Death looked at Ethan as he spoke, not as a man describing the final moments of a pretty waitress on an existential level, but as a businessman stating facts.

"Go? As in die? Where is she going?"

"We'll get to that, but yes, die."

"Ok, how can anyone have more than one chance to die?"

Death looked at Ethan, meeting his eyes as best he could in the hazy brightness of the surrounding fire. "You get as many chances as you need to get it right," Death replied.

At first confused, Ethan considered the words Death was saying. Chances? Wasn't death just death? And how could anyone die *right*?

"Here, watch," Death said, turning back to Omally. He reached his hand out and lightly touched her elbow that she'd held up defensively. Ethan watched entranced, suddenly immune to the horror he was standing beside. Death at last had his full attention.

Once he touched her, light escaped her body like rising embers, rushing out of her skin and cutting through the brightness of their surroundings, holding Ethan transfixed as they moved. They poured out of everywhere, flying around like lightning bugs, clearly visible even in the midst of the flames, before disappearing into the walls, floor, and ceiling. Some even passed through Ethan's body, giving off a warm and loving sensation that felt as wrong as it did right. It reminded him of good times from when he was young, before drugs and ignorance took away everything he loved, including his childhood. His heart glowed with the warmth and love he felt. It made him sick. "Jesus…" Ethan whispered.

Death smirked. "Yeah, that part never gets old."

They continued to rush out of the stationary body, immune to the time-stopping powers of the Grim Reaper. After a few more moments the lights faded or floated away, and the somber moment passed. Death took on his more jovial look. "Poof, there, Omally is gone. Off to a bet-ter place, or at least I assume she would think it was. I'm ninety percent sure she'll like it. Feels good to make a dif-ference, doesn't it?"

"Gone? Gone where? What the fuck was that? Was that her soul escaping or something?"

"Hmm. *Or something* fits. Souls are a tough concept to describe, but if that makes you happy, sure, it was her soul, floating off and breaking up back to where it came from."

"Where does a soul come from? Or is this getting back into the *who do you work for* crap you didn't answer be-fore?"

"Later. First, we need to deal with this asshole…" Death nodded over into the kitchen, but Ethan couldn't see past the fire. He just continued to follow when Death walked in.

As they moved, Ethan flinched as the fire kicked up again briefly, whooshing around their bodies in quick spurts. Ethan closed his eyes. Although he didn't feel an-ything, it was still disconcerting to be standing in a fire. Then, just as soon as it started, the flames and noise stopped again.

Once more there was a shadow of a corpse that mate-rialized out of the conflagration. This one was of a larger man, clearly the cook that had shouted the warning. His clothes were gone, however, his skin seemed considerably better than Omally's despite being so close to the source of the explosion.

Death walked over and leaned on the burning cook as if he were a grotesque mannequin. "Ah, now this pile of dicks here is a problem, but nothing I haven't seen before. See, he liked to toss his kitchen knives like some kind of badass at that target over there." Death indicated the wall next to the large fridge that had an old cutting block nailed to it. Beside the block that had a number of smaller knives in it was a larger chef's knife that was buried in an exploding wall, fire rushing out of it both above and below. Death continued.

"He was trying to be Captain Cool Pants to impress our young waitress over there, despite being a gross, post-middle-aged breakfast cook with no true worldly ambition as well as a wife and two kids at home. I'm sure you two would have got on swimmingly. Today he opted to try tossing some of his bigger knives. He missed on the very first try, put it through the drywall, and straight into the gas pipe behind the wall. Half the room filled with gas before he realized it and tried to shout out. Then the gas hit the closest burner on the stove, and here we are wandering through the eighth circle of Hell."

"Seventh," Ethan corrected.

"I'm sorry, did you just correct Death Himself as to which ring of Hell has the burning pit of fire?"

"Yeah, I did. Ring seven, the Ring of Violence, casts those who act against their neighbors…"

"Holy *fuck!* Fine, oh Great Lord of the Millennial Emos. Whatever. Dante was a prick, anyway. Because of this fat, lusty bastard, the life of our precious flower back there just got snuffed out. And he, unfortunately, is too stubborn to realize what he's done. Here, step back. This is going to go quick." Death pushed Ethan back against the wall far from where the gas explosion was sourced. Time seemed to start up again as they entered the kitchen. At first it flowed normally, and then it started going faster, as if picking up speed to catch up to the moments it had lost.

Ethan's head ached as he saw the world around him rush by. He had scant images of items and people being blown backwards, fire rushing around him, and walls ripping themselves apart. Kitchen items flew around them, some even passing through them like they were ghosts. Ethan couldn't bring his head around it all and hoped it would be over soon.

Then, everything seemed to be normal, albeit with an entire breakfast diner on fire and a man screaming on the floor beyond where they were standing. "I tweaked things a little once again, just so you know. It's better if we watch this next part uninterrupted."

Two middle-aged women ran into the building, shouting desperately for anyone to answer them. They were dressed in running attire and had panicked looks on their faces. They apparently didn't see an unscathed Death and shaken Ethan exit the kitchen through a newly created hole in the wall. "They can't see or hear us. Watch them, though. This is important." Ethan did as he was asked.

Incredibly, the charred form of the cook was moving on the floor, somehow still alive despite being at the epicenter of the blast. One of the women rushed over to him while the other found an extinguisher and started putting out what fires she could. After a few minutes, Ethan heard the familiar sound of the firetrucks that he'd heard more than once tearing up this main drag.

The woman tending the cook was speaking to him calmly, though what they were saying was still a mystery. Death walked over and stood beside them just as the first wave of firefighters burst in, screaming something at the two women. Time stopped again.

"Now take a looky here, my young squire." Death indicated the unfolding scene all around them while Ethan still tried to grasp what was happening. A lot had occurred in the last five minutes, and it was only now rushing into his head. "This extremely kind woman is Greta. Greta is a married, middle-aged housewife who was out for a morning run with her sister, who moments from now is going to be the first to discover the unfortunate body of our dear Omally, but we don't need to be around for that.

"These two amazing Samaritans foolishly burst in here looking for survivors, and who does Greta find but our idiot cook friend, who as you can see is very much alive. Like a cockroach, or aged politician."

"Yeah, how is that possible?" Ethan asked. "He should have been blown to bits."

"Yes, but he didn't want to be."

Ethan looked at him incredulously. "Well no shit, but he still should have been."

Death sighed, exasperated. "You're missing the point. He wasn't. He had the will to live through that, so he did.

At least in this reality. By force of will alone, he overcame tragedy. Sound familiar?" Ethan remained silent.

"Now, the gentleman, who we'll refer to as Stupid Cook since he doesn't deserve his real name right now, will endure years of aftereffects of this explosion. He will live in a hospital bed for months. He will undergo skin grafts and physical therapy so intense it would make your eyes water. More than once he'll wish he was dead, but he doesn't actually mean it. It will also be the greatest thing that has ever happened to him."

"Oh, clearly," Ethan answered, mocking looking around the destruction at their feet.

"I mean it, and I'll tell you why." Ethan looked at Death unbelievingly, but still listened. "Once the paramedics come and whisk Stupid Cook to the very same hospital you just spent a leisurely few nights at, Greta here will come for a visit to make sure he's alright. At that moment, these two will fall in love."

"I thought you said he was married with kids. She was, too."

Death cocked his eyebrow again and looked at Ethan like he was dealing with an indignant kindergartener. "Yes, because that's a thing that can stop love. A piece of paper and a party that costs too much money."

"What about the kids?"

"What about them? He loves his kids. Right now, he kinda sorta loves his wife, but he *loves* loves Greta after that moment. It's a kind of love they both never knew existed. At first it's confusing, and then it becomes more natural. Just over a year after today, they are both getting divorced and are dating each other. He loses child visitation for a time, but eventually gets it back. Greta has no kids, so she only leaves her husband. He doesn't take it well and eventually self-destructs himself into a heart attack three years from now."

"Jesus..." Ethan says, rolling his eyes. "What the fuck kind of story is this?"

"A true one, and one that isn't so farfetched if you have any familiarity at all with human emotions — which I admit you likely do not — so keep listening. I'm getting to my point. So, Stupid Cook and Greta get married, eventually move to Idaho where they live on a ranch, a dream they both have always had. He takes over as head chef, and she helps him in the kitchen. They find happiness, or at least as much as they can. That's when Stupid Cook will die."

"Why? What causes it?"

"It's different in every permeation of the universe, but the point is it happens, years after it should have, but only because he finally accepts that he should be dead. He carried on in his own world because he believed he had to. A part of him felt that he had unfinished business. Unfinished enough that he could survive this terrible day.

"Eventually the guilt over his foolishness today consumes him. He gives every dime he can spare to Omally's family, which by that point isn't chump change, and makes his peace with his stupid, chauvinistic decision that ended up costing a bright young waitress her life. Stupid Cook finally becomes Arty Spence in our story, and he dies peacefully in his sleep seventeen years from now.

Greta supports his decision after he admits to the cause of the explosion, and she outlives him by a number of years. He finds his peace. He makes it himself. I don't take him today like I did Omally. I take him seventeen years from now, which is a lot sooner than you might think."

Ethan looked around confused, but he was starting to piece it together. "So, you won't take them until they're ready."

"That's right. The lightbulb has started to glow, I see. Human will is an amazing thing. It can survive car accidents, drowning, kitchen explosions..." Death looked at Ethan and raised an eyebrow, "...plane crashes," he trailed off.

Ethan looked at Death surprised. "What do you mean by that?"

Death just shrugged. "Just what I said. Incredible as it may be to believe, your strength of will actually survived a massive horrifying plane crash. A crash that killed everyone else on board. Everyone else on that plane accepted their fate, because something like a massive plane crash into Puget Sound isn't something you walk away from. Every man, woman, and sadly, child on that plane acquiesced to the fact that their time had come. For some it was their third or fourth go round at trying to die. There was one guy at the back who was a thrill-seeker with a list of dark secrets that was up to twelve attempts at kicking the bucket. For others, mostly the children, it was their first, like Omally. And then there's you, who walked away while one hundred and thirteen others became universal vapor. Well, actually you swam, not walked. Whatever."

Death stepped away from the crouched form of Greta and Stupid Cook/Arty Spence, and time snapped forward again, but Ethan barely noticed it. All he saw was Death move towards the door.

After a moment of quiet, foolish reflection, he rushed after him. The hustle and bustle of the street scene was nothing but white noise to Ethan now. He jogged up beside Death and matched his walking pace on the sidewalk, back towards his home, or at least where it would be in his own universe. "This is some pretty heady shit, man."

Death nodded. "This is just a sample platter. The entrees will blow your mind."

Ethan looked back once more at the scene of the burning diner, and then looked forward again. "What's next, Death?"

"Death? Are you coming around?"

"Well, I have to admit you are pretty convincing, even if you're wearing Crocs."

"I'm Death. I'm pretty difficult to ignore."

Chapter 7

The two odd companions carried on down the street until Death reached an intersection and crossed over, heading down a road that would bring them to a bayside park if Ethan remembered correctly. Ethan was still in a state of shock from what he'd just witnessed. The explosion. The burnt bodies. The strange lights that poured out of the pretty waitress and made him feel things he'd long thought forgotten. Holden cars. Fucking *caddles*! God, they were gross… So much to process, and it was barely eight thirty. He clearly had not had enough coffee at that diner.

Death led the way, striding confidently in his stupid Crocs, unseasonable board shorts, and turtleneck that was actually quite practical in this weather but just ended up looking stupid when compared with everything else. He had a destination, and at this point Ethan was content just to wait and see how this was going to play out.

Eventually Death slowed, still with his grey eyes facing forwards, his destination up ahead. "So, I'm betting you have questions…" he said. Ethan couldn't tell if he was being serious or not. Obviously he had questions. Better to start slow.

"Damn right I do, so let's get started: You say people need to die *right*. How many chances does someone get? Is there a limit?"

Death smirked, "No, no limit, but it is true that some people just really suck at dying."

"What's the most you've ever seen?"

"What? Really? That's what you want to know? I'm DEATH, man! I hold the infinite complexity of the universe in my head and you want to trade baseball card stats? Man, you're depressing, but whatever, it's your time: one thousand six hundred and ninety-nine. That one is a particular pill."

"Seventeen hundred times he defied death? And he's still going? Who the hell is that?"

Death looked off into the distance as if he was seriously pondering the right words to say. It was an oddly introspective moment from someone Ethan had perceived as always having the right words. "He's a powerful man from another world. A world you wouldn't believe existed if I just thrust you into it. Hilariously enough, he ties into my reason for hiring you, but we'll leave that alone. Let's say that's too big a bite to take this early in the meal."

Ethan realized Death was right: facts and figures weren't interesting. Christ, why did he always have to think so small? "Alright, let's get back to Emily…"

"Omally," Death corrected.

"Right, sorry, Omally. What was that stuff that came out of her when you touched her arm? Those crazy warm lights?"

"Ah, a more intelligent question, but not one with an easy answer. I oversimplified by letting you call it a soul earlier, but it's closer to say that it was Omally herself."

Death Dresses Poorly

Clearly not a strong enough answer for Ethan, Death looked at him more pointedly. "Alright, how about this: it was everything that made her life worthwhile. It was the physical representation of her soul, life force, fuckin' Chi, whatever you want to call it. Everything she absorbed from the universe that was worth making a decent human being. See, you're all just drifting along in your own little worlds, picking up experiences and clever stories and bad knock-knock jokes and shit. Everything you are is contained in a miniscule amount of electronic impulses that rush through your body. Every memory. Every videogame cheat code. Every love lost. If you ever want to blow your mind, just sit down and really think about what humans really are: chemicals and electricity, all made up of atoms that can't touch, and will explode if broken. It's nuts."

"Yeah, I've had these conversations before. My old Chicago friends used to try to get deep into that shit when they got high."

Death thrust his hands out and looked to the heavens. "Again with the clichés. 'High people pondering the universe'. What's wrong with dropping X and fucking like rabbits like God intended? Stop wasting time pondering things you'll never possibly understand."

"God intended us to have crazy ecstasy sex?"

"God intended a lot of things you all fucked up. That's just one on a loooooong list. Think about it. He made a chemical that makes sex better! And yet here you are taking tabs and listening to shitty music. God is weeping, I swear to you."

"Ha, so there *is* a God!" Ethan smiled for a moment, before the crushing reality of what the statement meant hit him like a truck.

"Oh, don't look so lost in the abyss. God, or at least what you think of as God, doesn't exist and never has, but God as an entity sure as shit did. You all just misread the story since you were never around for it."

"Did? He's not around anymore?"

Death looked slightly down and his pace slowed. "He did. That's all I'll get into with that. When you take the job, you'll get it. All will be revealed." Death looked up and resumed his pace.

"Alright, that's a nice politi-speak non-answer, but I'm on a roll, so let's get to this: where did all those little floating things go? When Omally died? They had to have had a destination."

Death smiled his now-trademark grin and looked back at Ethan. "That is an excellently timed question, because that's the next place we visit. Or at least, you will."

"What do you mean me? What about you?"

"I'm not sure my being there would help or hinder your interpretation of the experience, so I'll likely bow out."

"Is it Heaven?" Ethan asked quietly. Images of suddenly seeing his mother in some stereotypical cloud world came to his head. Not that he hadn't seen her head in a cloud more than once, but it was usually grayish and had a distinct skunky smell to it. That was one of the great things about his mother; although it was an OD that killed her, she was always an equal-opportunity addict when it came to the narcotic world. Any high would do in a pinch. In retrospect, it was likely that indecisiveness that had killed her.

"Ha! No, Heaven is definitely not what it is. The sooner you people get over the concept of some glorious afterlife and realize that the truth is so much grander, the better we'd all be, but I know that's never going to happen. You idiots just can't let it go, even if it's what you should do. No, this place is a bit bigger in scope than something as measly as Heaven."

"Well," replied Ethan, "that's good, I guess."

Death looked at him. "An interesting retort to suddenly hearing that Heaven isn't real. Why do you say that?"

"Because if there's no Heaven, there's no Hell. I for one feel pretty fucking good about that."

Death stopped, almost causing Ethan to walk into him, but he caught himself and stepped back before the impact. Death turned to look at Ethan intensely, but not with anger. More so with something Ethan, if he didn't know any better, could have described as fear. A shiver ran up his spine at the thought so he pushed it away immediately. If this asshole really was Death, Ethan didn't even want to know what could possibly scare him.

Sensing the sudden change of mood, Death tried unsuccessfully to smile, but the look of something darker stayed in his eyes. "That's a pretty interesting way of thinking for someone so prone to negativity and malaise. Too bad I can't say it's true."

Ethan went white. "You… You're saying Heaven isn't real, but Hell is? That seems pretty fucked-up if you ask me."

Death looked down and sighed. "Look, I don't expect you to see the big picture so soon, but trust me when I say that eventually this will all make sense. Hell, or at least your idea of it, is as real a place as any you've ever been. But, it also isn't, and it's so much worse than that. Just as Heaven is too small an idea for the real endless glory, so is Hell. You and every other creature with a concept of these ideas still think way too small. In this instance, that's a good thing."

Ethan didn't know what to say, so he felt it was best to let it go. He wasn't in the mood for earth-shattering revelations about the nature of the afterlife. There was silence for a moment.

"Look," said Death, cutting through the awkward tension, "this is some pretty heady stuff, so let's just keep moving on down this path. Maybe it will all be clearer when we get there. Wow, that's a crap answer, isn't it? And I was the best Death for this job in all the cosmos. Fucked-up, right?" Ethan didn't answer.

Death turned back around and continued walking. Ethan, eager to escape the strange moment, was quick to follow.

They reached the park at the end of the road, which stretched out into the waters of Puget Sound, specifically Elliot Bay. Not exactly Ethan's favorite place in the world at that moment. He hadn't been near the water since he'd been pulled out of it covered in soap, and only now did the memories of the crash rush back to him. Death continued, striding though the green space and looking out at the strangely calm water. "So, back to the scene of the crime, eh?"

Ethan only sneered as he stood back from the water, tentative and afraid *(shit, so this is PTSD)*. "I guess. I'd rather be looking at it from far away, thanks."

"Hey, I get it. No hard feelings about manipulating the universe into trying to kill you, right? Bygones and all that?"

"Go fuck yourself."

"Ok, still tender. I gotcha. Anyway, staying back there isn't really an option. Also, you may want to have a seat or brace yourself or something. This is going to get weird."

Ethan crossed his arms. "Try me."

Death looked back out at the water. "Ugh… such a cliché."

Ethan wasn't sure what to expect, but it certainly wasn't what he got. Time didn't stop, but it didn't really continue to keep its straight and uniform line forward, either. He saw a bird flying above them slow to a strange crawl across the sky until it eventually froze. The lapping waves coming in off the water started to speed up at the same time, until they were eventually a blur that emanated a low wash of white noise Ethan couldn't say he had ever heard before. A tree blowing in the wind next to him suddenly started growing to an unbelievable size, and he watched it climb towards the sky in a great rush, narrowly missing the frozen bird. It caused him to stumble backwards and fall on his ass. He didn't even care.

All around him the benches and trees, waves and pathways, everything he could see, began stretching and distorting, all moving at their own speed as if they weren't all a part of the same world. A boat Ethan could see out on the water suddenly stretched like an elastic band on the horizon until its features were indistinguishable. Grass started to twitch underneath Ethan's hands and he pulled them up as if he were resting them on writhing worms. Some blades moved quickly, almost too fast for him to see, whereas others were locked in place. Everything around him was either in erratic motion, or unnaturally frozen in place. Distant things started to compress or elongate like accordions being pushed and pulled apart. Everything moved at a different speed.

Then other trees followed the lead of the first one, erupting up into the air, stretching as if trying to reach the sun itself. Shadows cast over the area everywhere as they grew, giving the already dreary day a nighttime feeling.

Panicked, Ethan looked at Death, who was still staring soundlessly out at the water. A feeling took hold in Ethan's stomach, as if he was suddenly weightless at the top of a rollercoaster parabola. If he wasn't sick before at the sight of the burned bodies, he was certain he was going to be now.

Death raised his arms and the hectic blur of the bay in front of them started to settle, carving a wide pathway of undisturbed water that led away from shore. All around it the water still banged and crashed at reckless speed, but this one gap cut through it until the water that occupied it became as still as glass.

The towering trees now formed a tunnel that blocked out only the forward view to Ethan. The grass still twitched, but it wasn't as unsettling a feeling as it had been before. Ethan just watched in amazement as the pathway in the water led away, as if it were an ice road to who knew where. Wind rushed all around him in the tree-tunnel now, disturbed by all of the irregular activity of reality.

The water started to fall away from the shore, but did not recede as Ethan expected. It actually dropped, as if it were being lowered slowly on a massive elevator. Only the serene water pathway remained, leading out from the mouth of the tunnel where Death stood. The daylight that had been pouring into the entrance became a warm reddish color. Despite the light, Ethan couldn't make out the clouds that had coated the sky when they arrived. It simply appeared to be blackness. The source of the light was unseen.

At last, the erratic universal movement stopped, and something resembling regular time took hold again. Death lowered his hands, but continued to look out at the place where Elliot Bay had just been. He said nothing.

Ethan slowly stood, reaching out to the woody tunnel walls for stability. Once he touched the side, a feeling of immense power rushed through his body, as if holding an electrical wire that surged with pure light. His brain was instantly confused. It was so unnatural, and yet it felt like the most natural thing in the world. Out of confusion, he pulled away quickly.

"You'll get used to that feeling. It's disorientating at first," Death said.

Ethan looked at his hand, not seeing any damage, although he wasn't sure there was supposed to be any. "What was that? What was disorientating?"

Death looked back slowly. "Everything, Ethan Dessier. That was the feeling of everything. A muted version of it, I grant you, but yeah." He turned back around and stared back out to whatever was beyond the tunnel, cast in that strange red light. He waved his right hand forward, indicating he wanted Ethan to join him.

Ethan was spellbound and speechless. He saw the crystalline pathway that had formed from the bay stretch out before him, and he was positive he could still hear water rushing, but he remained where he was. Death sighed again, clearly exasperated. "Look, this place is a lot more than Australian cars and caddles, I grant you that, but it's still only a sample of the whole thing. If you're really coming around to the strange truths, I guaran-damn-ty you won't learn anything in there. C'mon, sunshine. Let's broaden your mind for a moment."

Ethan was terrified. There was no getting around that fact. However, he was also curious as fuck. What had happened? Where was that light coming from?

Then, as if realizing his location anew, he looked backwards. Was this a tunnel, or just a weird tree cave? It appeared to be an actual tunnel, made up of solid walls comprised of tree trunks and pressed branches. He focused on the path behind him, looking for a sign of anything other than blackness. In an instant he was overcome with a sickening empty feeling. It created a void within his body that made him even more scared than he was before. The memory of the strange but not unpleasant feeling he had when he touched the tunnel wall was sucked from him like iron filings towards a magnet. He pulled his eyes away, but the gross empty feeling remained.

"Touch the wall again," Death said.

"Huh?"

"The wall. Touch it like you just did. It won't make it better completely, but it'll sure be an improvement."

Wanting the feeling gone as quickly as he could, he leaned into the wall and waited. Just as it had been taken from him, the strange warm feeling began filling the gap the cold emptiness had left. The memory of it, however, firmly remained.

"The memory never goes away. Sorry. There was no easy way to do that, so I just kinda let it happen. No way to help it. If I told you not to look back, there would have been no stopping you because you humans always do what someone tells you not to, and then you'd harbor some stupid grudge against me and all that. Bah. Might as well learn for yourself."

"Learn what?" Ethan called out in anger. He realized the tunnel contained no echo; only the sound of his breathing and the distant sound of rushing water. He walked towards Death, not wanting to take his hand off the wall in fear that the feeling would come back. "What the fuck is back there?"

82

"Oh, it's nothing…" Death replied. Ethan waited for him to finish speaking, and then he realized he was actually done. *Nothing* described the memory of that feeling better than anything he could have chosen. He started to think it was a carefully chosen word on Death's part. "You can take your hand away. So long as you don't look back again, you'll be good."

"*Good* is a pretty inept word, I'd say." Ethan stood next to Death, but only stared at the ground. He was scared to look up, either forward or back. There were too many new emotions in each direction. "What the fuck is back there, man?"

"Back there is a place that the name Hell can't even begin to describe."

"Geez, well then let's build a fucking tunnel that leads right to it! Makes sense. A great place to get away for a while. What the fuck is wrong with you? Why leave a thing like that around?"

"It predates me, kid. And I don't mean me the squirrel. I mean me as in Death. It goes back to the start of everything, and it's so much bigger than even I can imagine."

"So if that's back there, then what's out there?" Ethan indicated the end of the tunnel, seemingly only twenty or thirty feet away, but with all of the strangeness around them it was hard to tell.

"Out there is your destination. Out there is the opposite of what's back there."

That sounded appealing to Ethan, and curiosity was slowly getting the better of him. Oh well. No time like the present. He stepped past Death and began walking towards the end of the tunnel. His eyes started to process what he was seeing. The smooth pathway looked like glass, and all around it was a starry black that came more and more into focus.

And then Ethan emerged, and his breath was sucked from his body in pure awe.

Up and to his left was what looked like the sun, only it was so much closer, and it was tinged a deep red. It was this red super-giant that cast the odd light everywhere. Just ahead, the place where the bay had been when it fell away was now a precipice into oblivion, however, the edges of the pathway ahead poured water downward like a cascading waterfall that dropped into nothing. Ethan couldn't see where the water was going, but he knew as he crept closer that he couldn't make out a bottom of any kind.

He looked up and back at the entrance to the tunnel. The trees were still there, reaching towards the red sun, but they were gigantic. Like mountains with roots, making him realize how a bug must feel next to a sequoia. Death stood motionless, watching Ethan take everything in.

The sky beyond the glare of the redness was full of an array of planets and smaller stars. To his left and right, where the shoreline had been before, was an endless beach that fell into the abyss. Washington State was far away from wherever this was.

Death still remained in the tunnel. "You coming?" Ethan asked.

Death shook his head. "No. My place is here. You take a look around. I'll be here when you get back. I recommend following that fancy path there."

"Bullshit, I'm not going anywhere. Not without you, anyway."

Death held his hands over his heart and fluttered his eyes at Ethan. "Aww, I'm touched that we've grown so close in just a morning. Sorry, I won't go out there. I stay here. Come back if you want, but you'll be missing out on something I can personally attest to being one of the greatest moments of your existence."

Ethan looked back out down the seemingly never-ending path that drifted off into the stars. "Will it be hard to get back?"

Death shook his head. "As easy as apple pie. Just try to come back, and poof, here you'll be."

The temptation, not to mention the fulfilling feeling he got when he looked down the shining path, was too much for Ethan to resist. It filled a hole in his existence he didn't know he had. "Alright, I'll see where this takes me, but if I can't take it, you better stop and take me back when I tell you."

"Ha, I'm sorry, but Death doesn't have a safe word, princess. This is one trip you won't want to come back from. I'm betting you'll be pretty pissed off when you see me again because that means it'll be over."

Ethan severely doubted that was true. Not the being pissed off to see him part, but the fact that this would be a journey with a pleasing result. Even in the midst of all this wonder, he didn't trust Death in the slightest. "Not wanting to see you again, eh? Sounds terrible. How will you know when I need to come back?"

"I bend all worlds to my will. I see, know, and control everything."

"Ooo, and you're super humble, too. Nice."

"Look, smartass, just go. Take a walk down that pretty little path, and I'll see you when you're done to take you for your next lesson."

"Right, right. The infinite complexity of the universe. That's what you said, wasn't it? Back in Chicago?"

"Good memory. Yes, Ethan. That very thing, though I'm betting you'll have a pretty good idea once you get back from your little galactic stroll." Death waved once and gave a cheery false-smile. "Have fun!"

"Don't you know by now? I'm not a big fan of fun."

"Jeez, I am mystified how you even function on a daily basis."

"Easy. My fuel cells run on snark and skepticism."

"Fuck, if that's the case, you aren't ever coming back. You'll walk on forever."

Ethan turned back to the road ahead. "Is this really safe?"

Death looked thoughtful before replying. "Safe? No, but it's worth it."

Chapter 8

Ethan couldn't explain why he wasn't tentative about stepping onto the bizarre, opaque walkway with water pouring off each side into nowhere as far along as he could see, but he never hesitated when he first walked out. A solid ground met his feet, and he simply put one in front of the other and headed out.

The sides were a bit disconcerting, with no railings or protective barriers stopping him from falling off into what appeared to be an unfathomable abyss, but after all the strangeness that had happened to him in the last week, Ethan didn't think he'd suddenly wander off an edge. If he stayed in the center and kept his eyes forward, there was nothing to fear. Besides, Death had said that when he wanted to come back, he could, so logically that meant even if he was plummeting into the nothingness below.

Ha! "Logical"? That was a fucking laugh. There was nothing logical about what had been happening. Ethan actually smiled to himself as he walked on, not out of humor as much as it was from lunacy. This whole situation was madness. No, better yet, this whole situation was just a dream. It was a vivid one, and he was likely still drugged out in a hospital bed just waiting to wake up. Having never been one for opiates and other harsh pharmaceuticals, he had no idea if this was what happened when doped up. Ugh, it probably was. That said, he never thought he possessed this vivid an imagination.

God, this was so fucking weird. He looked back briefly. The massive towering trees still loomed over him, but the image of Death standing in his stupid shorts just beyond the tunnel entrance grew smaller and smaller. Death waved sarcastically, and he could feel that stupid smile from here, so naturally Ethan flipped him off in response.

Foolishly, he briefly looked beyond the asshole in the tunnel and saw past him. At once that emptiness returned, nauseating him and crippling his guts with pain. He doubled over, placing his hand on the ground to balance himself. The roadway felt like soft glass moments from shattering, but that deep peace he had felt back in the tree tunnel returned, filling him back up enough to feel empowered.

"Don't look back there!" he heard Death shout, though he'd have sworn he was too far away to be heard so clearly. Ethan only shook his head, stood, and headed back along. *No shit, Sherlock.*

The huge red sun hung over his left shoulder and illuminated the immediate surroundings. The planets that hovered around in the distance spun silently, a cacophony of colors and swirls, sizes and shapes. It was quite possibly the most beautiful thing he had ever seen, but he also admitted to himself that that was a low bar to hurdle.

He wasn't sure how long he walked for, but he certainly didn't mind the journey in such a strange and wonderful place. He almost could tell, in the part of his brain so well attuned to detecting bullshit, that this was a façade, and he was ok with that. He didn't think this place meant him any harm. It was more of a chance to start expanding his mind without making it explode. A place to start his transubstantiate voyage, like a videogame hub world. Not that he had time for videogames beyond some basic ones he had on his tablet.

Ethan could feel the enormity of the space surround him as he traveled. He'd almost say he was wandering aimlessly, but the truth was that he had a very specific and direct aim in mind: he was here to test the limits of what it was that Death was saying. Was this really space? It seemed an odd thing to think, but he supposed it was possible. As the planets spun and the stars in the distance twinkled, it wasn't so far-fetched to imagine that every one of them was a different world, or even a thousand different worlds. Was every star home to more living things that needed Death?

More than once as he went, feet gliding along almost effortlessly, he swore he saw a shooting star streak by only to stop and freeze in place. They became one of the billions of stationary stars around him. Or at least, he thought they did. After a while it was entirely possible that Death was just playing tricks on him. Was this the kind of thing Death could do? Even cynical Ethan Dessier had to admit it was pretty cool, although it made him feel infinitely smaller. If every star was a home to billions, or even *trillions* of lives that lived and then died, who the hell was he now? If he was nobody in his own world, in endless worlds he could actually be even less.

Death Dresses Poorly

If he took the job, could he actually be more?

He may have been walking for hours, or maybe it was just minutes. The sound of his feet bouncing off the walkway was hypnotic, and a welcome escape from reality. Literally, actually. He simply wandered, waiting for something to happen, trying to avoid thinking about his miniscule place in all of this, while memories of the past started dripping into his consciousness, as they often did when he was alone for too long. He was strong, but not so strong that he could keep them at bay forever, even in a place like this. He was either consumed by the space, or consumed by his mind. His mind was currently the lesser evil since it was the one he knew best. His memories were full of pictures of a dirty house he endlessly tried to keep clean, hospital visits, and the occasional dinner out with his sister.

Christ, his sister. With the events of the morning he hadn't even thought about Arlene. If this Death thing was real, what would happen to her? She had flown out to see him, and she was a decent person, despite some past transgressions against his mother. She'd be alone.

Or would she? Could he pop in and visit? How did this work? He realized he hadn't even scratched the surface of what was going on.

He didn't have any answers, but that didn't make him want Death back quite yet. The thought of actually being *something* in all of this was certainly appealing, but he had no idea what the rules were. Would his consciousness be everywhere at once? Would he be able to look in on Arlene now and again? Would he still even carry on as

90

himself, or would Ethan the young man simply fade away? The thought was in his head now of Arlene crying if Ethan disappeared to take his new crazy job. Would she assume he killed himself? Shit, that would be terrible! She'd blame herself. There was no way around that. She'd be upset that she left when she did, and then what? Would she buck-up and carry on? It was possible, but he couldn't dismiss the thought that she might do something stupid. She was strong, but was she *that* strong? Or was he a fool to doubt it? He could only speak for himself, and even after the *Puget Plunge (*Copyright review underway) he didn't consider that kind of action. He wasn't exactly awash with the glory of life, but he wasn't suicidal either.

If he was Death, and his sister killed herself in a state of horrible depression, would he have to carry her soul away like that Omally chick? Or what if it was years from now and she died of old age? Would he feel anything as he did it? Would he even recognize her as his sister anymore?

Fuck. So much to think about. So much to ask Death about. He considered looking back again to see how far he'd come, but just looking back once was out of character for him. Twice was unthinkable. Ethan Dessier never looked back. There was always too much shit behind him to be reminded of.

He suddenly realized that while he was walking in his haze of what might happen to Arlene, the rushing sound of water had died away. He looked around, but even the edges of the pathway had faded from view. As strange as it was to see, he appeared to be walking through a vast empty space, but not actually walking on anything. To his surprise, he wasn't dizzy or disoriented. He did, however, stop and reassess his situation.

The red sun still burned and the planets still spun. Occasionally there would be a shooting star in the distance, and they really were stopping in some far off place. It was all very picturesque, but not terribly helpful. With no more paths and no set destination, he considered turning back.

When he dejectedly decided to look behind him just to see how far he'd wandered while lost in thought, he gasped audibly when he saw the Earth about the size of a beachball. Although clearly Earth, something was different. It was swirling and changing. He could see the coastlines of Africa and India move and shift, while the coloration of the land masses swayed, taking on almost every hue of the spectrums he could see. The globe was awash in a Technicolor dream, like soap bubbles. The oceans seemed to drain and refill. Lakes formed and cut continents in half, and then they would recede, and the world would look like it was supposed to. Or at least, what Ethan assumed it looked like. He had an image in his head of what the Earth should look like, but he wasn't exactly a geographer.

Ethan stared wide-eyed at the strange scene, and for the first time since he stepped out onto the water-formed walkway, he began to feel fear. He was suddenly reminded of the plane crash. That crippling, falling terror was back in full force.

"Don't worry," came a soft voice behind him. "He's just enigmatic like that. You didn't really go that far."

Ethan spun, surprised at the words. He looked back the way he came and was instantly confronted with the face of his mother. Shock overtook him and his feet stumbled in a tangle of confusion. He fell backwards and braced himself for hitting the ground, but the ground never came, and he fell backwards while tumbling into the nothingness.

He shut his eyes, and he could feel the wind (wind in space?) rush past his ears. *No,* he thought, *no no no. Not this. Not falling. Not again!* He tried to scream, but he couldn't even control his mouth to make a sound. He was frozen, except for his eyelids which he refused to open in fear of what he may see.

His brain suddenly flashed to an unfamiliar memory: that of the plane heading for the water. His head had been knocked hard enough that he didn't remember any of the crash itself, but that apparently didn't mean the memory was deleted. It was still in there, just waiting for the chance to be reactivated. That time had come.

He saw an oval shape he knew to be an airplane window, and outside was an ever-charging water surface. Always getting closer. Always right there, about to end his life.

Only it didn't, did it? He survived that crash. Or did he? Maybe he didn't *die right,* but maybe he did? How did he know if he was even alive anymore and this was just part and parcel of the experience of casting off the mortal coil?

"It's not, you know," said his mother's voice in his ears, as if she was still right in front of him, even while he twisted and fell through the nothingness. "You're still alive. Being alive is what makes you so special."

"SHUT UP!" he finally got out, but it was all he could manage. Still no scream.

"No," the voice continued, "I won't. I'm here to help. Quick, tell me, what's a good memory you have of me?"

"Fucking dying and leaving me alone!" Ethan shouted, still seeing the water rushing up to his face about to claim one hundred and thirteen lives. Only this time it would be one hundred and fourteen. He couldn't survive this again...

"Ethan, listen. Think back. Find it. What do you remember? The only memory you need is the one you'll find. One good one, you and me."

"You didn't give me any! Go away!"

"Ethan," she said again, sternly but lovingly, which wasn't a tone he could ever remember her using: the tone of a real mother and not a fuck-up, "just one."

The water was getting closer. He didn't open his eyes, but he could feel it. He tensed and braced himself.

"Just. One."

Ethan forced his brain away from the incoming wall of water and thought hard. He had no reason to, but he had no reason not to, either.

The water was getting closer. This was about to end badly.

"Ethan…"

"Aaaarg *alright!*" Ethan suddenly shouted, finding something deep in the recesses of his brain.

All at once he felt his momentum shift. It was unsettling and strange, turning his sense of direction for a loop, and he could feel himself getting whisked along in a different direction than straight down. He was pushing forwards now, and the sound of rushing water was back, only it was different. It was louder and more intense.

He opened his eyes and was surprised to find that he was back in a tunnel. His body was curving left and right, occasionally going over a hill that made his stomach lurch. After a few moments, he began rushing for a bright light at the end. He was about to fall out into space…

…Only it wasn't space. It was a splashdown pool. He was in a waterslide.

He hit the warm water with a rush and was under in an instant. His clothes weighed him down, but his feet hit the bottom and he stood up, with fresh air meeting his face as he sputtered and spit. He wiped the water away from his eyes and squinted, looking out at where he suddenly found himself.

Once his eyes were open completely, the sound of water stopped. The silence returned, and he was bone-dry standing on the bottom of an empty pool.

He was dumbfounded. What had just happened? He could see beyond the empty wave pool in the distance, and beyond that was more of the special emptiness just as it was before. The red sun still burned on.

"See. I told ya!" came a more familiar tenor voice from behind him where the tunnel emerged. "Wasn't that one of the greatest moments of your existence? What a ride!"

Ethan turned quickly, seeing Death leaning on the fiberglass tube a few feet away. "Wha... What the fuck was that?!?!"

"That, my dour companion, was a jacked-up waterslide. Truly a most thrilling attraction."

"Oh, shut up! What *was* that? The empty space? Falling? My *mother*?!?!"

"That was your trip. Your experience. Your way of getting here, to the glory that is *here*. Every life finds a new path when they arrive. Yours was just terrifying and full of crazy images and a dead mother, though I suspect that part may actually have been real. Most just fly here or are carried aloft on golden chariots, but I guess those were never really your style. Even here, you apparently need to torture yourself. Figures. Maybe it's because you're still technically alive? Living people never come here."

Ethan jumped up on the edge of the empty pool and stomped over to Death, murder in his eyes. Death held his hands up defensively. "Whoa whoa, mister. Not a good idea trying to get rough with the Ageless Stranger. That's how bad things happen."

"You had better start talking!" Ethan demanded. "I thought you said you couldn't go out of that tunnel, and I would find you later?"

"And you did. See, I was right. And about the tunnel thing, I can go anywhere I like. Besides, I never said I couldn't. I said I *won't*. That was your trip to take. You had to find this place on your own, and when you did, I would follow. So I followed. Where is *here,* anyway?"

The fire died down behind Ethan's eyes, but the rushing heart and heavy breathing remained. He should have fucking known it. He should have seen this trick coming from a mile away. Why would Death play fair? Still, his mother, or at least a much cleaner and nicer version of her, was certainly real. He didn't dream that. "You are such an asshole…"

"Granted, so yeah, where are we?"

Ethan sighed and looked around. He hadn't been here in years, but he still knew it well. It was surprising how well he remembered this place. "Mystic Waters, just outside of Chicago. I used to come here when I was a teenager with my friends to get away from my mom."

"Funny, this doesn't look like an angsty teenage hangout."

Ethan's rage began to subside, and his heartbeat slowed now that the ride was over. "It wasn't. Or at least, we pretended it wasn't. We'd come here pretending it was stupid and ironic when really we just wanted to play and have fun. Especially me. My mother's situation was common knowledge for most of high school."

"You hung out at a water park to be dark and cool? Teenagers are weird."

"It's like seeing a bunch of teenagers on a grade school jungle gym, right? They're pretending to be so mature and 'ironic' being there, when actually they just want the joy of spinning really fast and playing a game of Grounders again, trying to forget their childhood is passing them by."

"Jesus fuck, kid. That's some deep shit, even for you."

Ethan shrugged. "I knew it right away; the subterfuge, right? No one cared and I never mentioned it. I just wanted to have fun."

"So, that's why we're here? To remind you of your shitty teen years?"

Ethan thought about it, now convinced more than ever that despite what Death had said, this totally *was* some crazy "Christmas Carol" shit. Still, he played along. "No, we're here because of my mother."

Ethan took a heavy breath before he began. He hadn't thought about the feelings he was about to discuss in ages. "There was a time, when I was almost ten, where my mom had just started to really dive into the pit she died in. After her first nasty binge, Arlene and I were sent to stay with some cousin we'd never met and didn't know, but was the only family we had around. When we got back, Mom swore she was going clean. She swore she didn't want to lose us and she would do better. It was her first go-'round on the hard shit and we were so young, so Arlene and I believed her. She went for about a week and everything was just as it had been, pretty good, right? At least, as good as it could be after Dad left. Oh shit... this isn't one of those 'Death is actually my dad' M. Night Shayamalan twists, is it?"

Death burst out laughing, a sound that was loud but didn't echo in the empty space of the fake amusement park all around them. "Ha! Oh sweet lord, no. No Ethan,

I'm not your dad. Your dad was a deadbeat who took off when he got cold feet and thought he'd found something better. Married again. No kids. Wife is a bitch. Lives down south somewhere I think. Still, my personal opinion, without looking into the magic glass of the eons, is that you were still better off without him, mom's death and all."

Ethan took the information in, but wasn't surprised to find that he didn't really care. He wasn't starry-eyed at the thought of ever finding his dad, though his leaving almost certainly triggered his mother's depression and eventual drug use. "Oh, thank God. Well, anyway, after a few weeks I think she started to slip again and got scared, so she tried to give herself a slap to straighten out by bringing Arlene and I here for a day. We all played, all three of us, like a real family. My sister and I had so much fun, and I think my mom did, too. Years later when I looked back on it, I remember her being distant. Not emotionally, but *actually* distant. She was walking away and looking back at us while we had fun, like she was trying so hard to take a mental image of happiness to help get her through. Then the day ended, we went back home, and soon after she fell back into using. The rest is history. We never went back as a family, but we honestly had such a great day."

"Was it the greatest day of your life?"

"Well 'Surviving a Plane Crash Day' needs to be right up there, not to mention 'First Back-Alley Hand Job'…"

"You know what I mean."

Ethan turned in a rage, refusing to give Death the satisfaction just in case a tear or two showed up. "I don't know, man! Maybe… I guess so. It's a blur. I just know that I had so much fun here that day, with the promise of a happy mother and repeated trips to the water park that never ended up happening until I was older and way more jaded and Arlene had left home. I had hope, then. Like a kid is supposed to. Hope that the Scary Mommy would be gone and things were actually going to be alright. So just now, when my phantom mom told me to find a good memory of her, this was it. Now I'm here, standing on a space-island shaped like a great and also horrible childhood memory, describing it to a guy who's apparently Death."

"*Apparently*? I had assumed my credentials were satisfied at this point."

"Not yet, boss. I still have questions. Fucking millions of them."

Death opened his arms wide, invitingly. "Fire away. That's why I'm here."

Ethan felt like he was about to cry, but held back. He did have a million questions; new ones that were fully formed and needed answering, but only one mattered to ask right at this moment. "Was that really my mother?"

Death nodded, recognizing the importance and difficulty of the question. Even he knew when to dial it back. "Sorta. Sorry, that's not a great answer, but it's the best I can do right now. It may be closer to say it's the mother both you and she wanted her to be."

Ethan looked at him perplexed, waiting for more information to go on. Death looked like he was about to say something else, but stopped himself and started walking away. Normally this would have enraged Ethan, but after the morning he'd had, he opted to just follow Death and continue on this strange trip. A part of him had to accept that in a place like this there were no simple answers.

Death walked beyond where the little kids used to play and stopped just short of the drop off into the nothing of space, staring out to the red sun and whatever lay beyond. "What is this place?" Ethan asked as he came up beside him.

"That's a pretty generic question. What place?"

Ethan looked at Death incredulously. "*This* place! This space out in space! Why do I feel like I got lost in a bad Epcot Center ride?"

"Is there a good Epcot Center ride?"

"I don't know. Ask someone who's fucking been there, I guess. You know what I mean: like I'm stuck in the middle of a planetarium exhibit."

"Well I'll save you a trip: there's not. Epcot sucks. Anyway, this is like I said. This is Everything. Absolutely Everything. This is the physical representation of anything and everything that has ever been and ever will be. It's just funneled through a very simplistic lens in order to allow you to process what you're seeing."

"Can't say I've ever been into space and stars and shit. I mean, it's cool and all, but I'm not one for putting my head in the clouds."

"Ha. There's a plane crash joke in there somewhere." Ethan only glowered at Death. "Look, I'm new to this too. Death as an entity has no real basis on how to show the glory of everything to a set of human eyes. Especially ones that don't really want to see. Humans have very rarely been Death before, so this is new territory for everyone involved."

"Why? What's wrong with humans?"

"Are you serious? What *isn't*? You're irrational, sporadic, quick to anger, conflicted. What you would think of as *lesser* animals and life forms are so much easier to train to get into the role."

"Like squirrels?"

"You're god damned right like squirrels. We're majestic as fuck. We have a job to do and we do it. Quick. Efficient. Beautiful. All while being able to have a little fun. And, like, real fun. Fun for the sake of pure joy. Dolphin-style fun. Not fun in our time off, or fun to tell ourselves we're something we're really not, or fun for the sake of trying to escape our shitty life and decisions."

"Low blow, ass."

Death winked at Ethan and pointed his finger at him while clicking his teeth. "It's the only kind I deal, sport. Keep up. Anyway, humans don't make good *Death* as a general rule."

"Well that brings me to my next question: why me? What makes me so damn special?"

"Surviving a plane crash by sheer willpower and desire alone doesn't tip you off?"

"All it says is I'm too stupid to know when to die."

"Huh. That's a very interesting take on the situation. Well, like I said: something is about to happen, in a world you've never been to, with people you'd never believed could exist. It's going to be on a level the universe has never experienced before, and we're going to need some of that patented human tenacity and stubbornness to get through it. Refusing to die in an inescapable flying death machine seems to tell me that you're quite possibly the man the universe needs."

"Holy jeez, no pressure or anything."

"Well, actually there is a lot of pressure... oh, you were making a funny. Aren't you just so witty." Ethan couldn't tell if he was serious or not. He assumed not. It was the safer bet at this point in their relationship.

"Alright, so what's this thing that's going to happen? What is this grand and horrible disaster I'm supposed to prevent instead of going to work today?"

"Yeah, that would have been great. The photocopy girl was going to blow you in the bathroom."

Ethan went cold. "You better be fuckin' lying."

Death shrugged. "Well, you'll never know. And to answer your questions, we need to do something a few more times before you understand."

It was Ethan's turn to roll his eyes. "Let me guess: visit a few more strange realities with shitty fruit and languages I don't understand?"

"Good guess, but it's a little deeper and more gruesome than that."

Ethan nodded in understanding. "We need to kill a few more people."

"We have a bingo. Well, sorta. Like I said, Death doesn't do the actual killing. Death just sets the dying in motion. And it's not just people, though. There's a whole laundry list of entities out there that have passed their expiration dates. Time to get to work."

"Sounds good. Lead the way, Mr. Stupid Clothes."

Death actually looked offended and Ethan wondered if he'd gone too far. They really were stupid, though. "We're in a water park," he replied coolly but clearly irritated. "What the fuck was I supposed to wear? Boardshorts seemed appropriate."

"And the turtleneck?"

"To protect against that fucking Seattle February chill, obviously."

"And the Crocs?"

"Those are just here to piss you off."

"They're working."

"Of course they are. That's why they were invented. So, let's get marching. If you would kindly lead the way."

"Where?" Ethan asked before looking around and seeing a large ornate green door behind them. It was easily three times taller than either of them and had a massive golden handle on the side with dark carvings and images so miniscule that Ethan had a hard time making them out. "Nice door," he said, legitimately impressed.

"Thanks. A good door is hard to find. Now, let's see what's beyond it."

Ethan stepped forward, with no small part of him eager to open it and get away from this beautiful, horrible memory.

Chapter 9

Ethan took one last look around at the strange surroundings before grasping the large handle and attempting to pull the door open.

Death just smiled. "Push, stupid."

After pushing it and cursing at his host, Ethan stepped through the door and was instantly hit with an assault to his senses. Green flooded his eyes and a sweet, almost minty smell filled the air. The air was chillier than the strange space he'd come from, but not outright cold. He led the way, eager to get away from the good/bad memories of Mystic Waters.

He found himself inside what appeared to be a forest, with huge green trees looming overhead. They weren't as large as the ones that had grown around him on the beach back in Seattle, but they were no less impressive.

A scurrying noise shook the air to his left, and he turned to see a massive yellow bug he didn't recognize loom over him with large eyes taking him in suspiciously while its mandibles opened and closed furiously, causing Ethan to step back and quickly look for cover. However, it simply ignored him and then carried on down a makeshift pathway.

"Damn, they grow'em big here, don't they?" Death said, smiling beside Ethan. "Might want to watch out. I hear they like to eat douchey millenials."

"What the fuck is that!?" Ethan shouted, suddenly realizing that the echo of sound had returned. It assaulted the area, bouncing around and hitting his ears multiple times while taking him by surprise. It was like going from sleep to a train wreck. Ethan suddenly and unsurprisingly concluded that he quite enjoyed the sound of absolute silence.

"That is a big yellow bug. Impressive, isn't it? Up close, you can really see the details."

"Fuck the details! Why is it so big?"

Death looked at him as if perplexed. "Big? It's the same as every other bug. Wait, you don't think you're in a forest, do you? Take a look around again."

Confused, Ethan did as he was asked, and almost immediately he picked up on what Death was saying. He wasn't in a forest; he was in a field of grass. He could see the tufted ends of the blades that had grown large and uncut. He also noticed a number of colorful flowers blooming high above him. It looked as though they were in a field somewhere. The grass was tall and not uniform, with round, strong stalks. "So, we're really tiny? Why?"

"All the better to enlighten you, my dear," Death said with a smile. "Follow me, please. Our next stop on the docket is through here." He indicated Ethan to follow him though a gap between sprouts.

Ethan stepped in line behind him and started paying closer attention to the world around him as they moved. That all-encompassing feeling of *everything* was still there, and he didn't need to be touching anything to make it fill him. There was so much life here, and he felt as if he could touch it all, and actually even more, which he couldn't explain. If he was really feeling life, what else could there be? Where was this other feeling coming from?

As the overwhelming joy of the moment wrapped around him like a warm heavy blanket, he had a sudden and unwanted reminder of the feeling at the back of the tunnel when he first entered. That nothingness that filled him so utterly. It made him feel sick.

"It'll keep doing that, you know," Death suddenly chimed in. "Whenever you get too full of all the glory, that emptiness will hit you like a stereotypical Southern husband. I wish I could say you get used to it…"

"Well thanks for letting that happen, man. I'm so glad to have that be a part of my life."

"Your sarcasm is really your best feature, you know that? You truly are a walking pile of negativity."

"Call it what you want. I'm still alive because of it, aren't I?"

Death briefly looked back at Ethan, apparently half-impressed, but said nothing. Ethan smiled, knowing he'd just trumped Death and hit him where it hurts, but also because Death didn't seem to mind the jab. One point for Ethan.

Eventually, Death continued, "It had to happen. You had to see the other side of things. There was no way I could allow a mortal like you to simply waltz into the glory of all existence without something to level you out. You'd fry a circuit, and the last thing you need lately is even more brain damage."

Ethan scowled at Death as he led the way. "No thanks to you, right?" Death didn't answer. "So, I need to forever experience this crippling void in my heart in order to keep going to all of these lovely places you take me? That's bunk, man. Why?"

"You can't have the wonder of everything without the grasp of nothing."

"Uh-huh. You serve the balance."

"I serve the balance."

They walked on a bit farther. Every now and then Ethan caught a glimpse of something moving in the distance; a large bug or some kind of bird high in the sky, but nothing else came close to them before they reached their destination. He was also careful not to take in too much of the majesty, as it were. He wanted to avoid that nothingness as much as possible, even though his heart started to ache for the peace and happiness that everything gave him.

Now that his ears were accustomed to sound again, he could hear the drone of distant cicadas, the chirp of crickets, and the unsettling rustle of something moving through the grass beyond their field of view. Death only led the way, seemingly unaffected by the tranquil scene around them. Silence was wonderful, but in the right doses Ethan found a place in his cold heart for this kind of all-natural white noise. Growing up in Chicago and its endless suburban sprawl, he never really had time for wandering through the wide open spaces the real Midwest offered. *Fuck*, he thought, *one little walk and I'm already going soft.*

Eventually they came out to a small clearing with a large thatch of grass growing in the middle. Half a dozen tree-like stems reached up towards the sky. Ethan approached them, passing Death as the tall man watched him.

"What do you feel?" Death asked. "Search whatever you call a soul and tell me what you sense in everything that surrounds us?"

Ethan didn't even need to ask Death what he was referring to. He could feel something the moment he approached the stalks. It wasn't horrible like the nothing feeling. It was bad, but bad in a different way. A more natural way, though even that feeling didn't make sense to him.

Death joined him next to the grass stems and pointed to a smaller stalk to Ethan's left. It was fresh growth, only half the height of the others, but still much taller than both of the travelers standing at its base. "I can tell you're starting to get attuned to the way things are. That's why we started so big, back at the walkway and waterfalls. It helped you figure out what was what. Touch that. See what you think."

"I'm not about to feel up a blade of grass."

"Humor me."

"Ha, that's not fuckin' likely. You've already proven to be a pretty untrustworthy guide. How about you touch it."

Death shrugged and stepped forward. Ethan remembered Omally from the diner and wondered if the result would be the same when Death touched the grass. When his black-clad host placed his hand on the green plant, nothing of note happened. Everything remained as it was.

"It's not about death this time. At least, not yet, and not exclusively. This is more about the balance. A balance this little guy here is doing his damndest to upset. C'mon, live a little. But, like, not really, since that goes against the whole plan I have for you."

Ethan cocked an eye at his companion, but still stepped forward to the growth that was easily twice as wide as his arm's width. He placed a hand next to Death's on the green stem. His body shook all at once as he could feel something writhing. The feeling wasn't coming from the surface, which was smooth and fibrous and felt like petting a bristly dog. The uneasiness came from inside. It wasn't a bug, but more miniscule than that. Something microscopic. It was unpleasant to feel, as if his brain had dipped itself into a bucket of night crawlers and none of them were happy to be there, but he didn't pull away. "Ugh, what is that?"

"That," he heard Death reply as he kept his eyes closed, "is known in the exciting circles of gardening enthusiasts as 'Fusarium Blight'. It's a grass fungus that thrives in drought conditions like the ones currently happening around us, though you wouldn't know it to see it." Ethan could hear Death step away, leaving him alone with his hand on the grass. "You see," said that annoying tenor voice, "that gross feeling is an unnatural intruder creeping into this wandering sprig of greenery and infecting our noble grassy friend here. Soon, it will infect every stem in this little group, and it will eventually kill them all. This is the first blade to be infected, deep down in its roots. The fungus is spreading. In time, it will take over the grass you see around us, killing it all as far as you can see and beyond, which will cause an unimaginable shift in the balance of life and death in this part of the near-infinite universes. For my job, and soon to be your job, that's catastrophic. The resources needed to fix an issue like this and its effect on the balance I strive so hard to maintain is unimaginable."

"Then fix it."

"Look, ass, if I could fix it I would. However, it's a living thing, and as we've previously discussed, that's rule #1: we can't kill anyone."

"Jesus, are you Death or the genie from *Aladdin*?"

Death removed his hand from the plant and stared daggers at Ethan. Once again, Ethan stood his ground. What was really to fear from an entity that just finished admitting he can't kill? The look was still terrifying, nonetheless. "This is fucking serious, kid, so listen well: Death does not kill. Death, as in the end of life, is an individual event in the finite lives of all living things. Death, that is to say me, only works to distribute the essence of the living, those things represented by glowing lights from the cute waitress eager to get all aboard your dick train, to where they need to be throughout the infinite expanse of everything in order to be the most productive. I can bend some rules to help maintain that balance, like creating a breeze that makes prey more easily found to its predator, or set in motion small events that lead to a bigger picture like a pile of gravel that makes some asshat in a Maserati

III

spin out and die, but *not* hit the mother and her new child ten miles down the road if that gravel wasn't there, which would have caused a massive imbalance in lifeforce that would have taken forever to clean up…"

"Or putting together a string of events to make a passenger jet drop into the cold-ass waters of Puget Sound?"

Death put his hands up as if captured by the police. "Aw, you got me. Yes, exactly like that, not to mention all the galactic wheeling and dealing that needed to be done to find enough balance for the lifeforce of all of the other one hundred and thirteen passengers aboard, or the *billions* of lives taken in the water itself. Fish, plankton, single-cell organisms killed by the jet fuel or fires, some of which were far more powerful and irreplaceable than some of the assholes on that plane in the grand scheme of things. But, all that said, the actual act of dying is a terribly personal thing, and one that I'm not involved in. It happens strictly without my involvement, once that particular life has made peace with the fact that it can no longer go on."

"Bullshit," Ethan answered, taking his hand away from the grass and removing that creepy, dark feeling from his brain. "What about that Omally girl? I saw you touch her and have that glowing stuff pour out of her."

"Ah, very astute. You're marginally not as dumb as you look, but only sometimes. That was me distributing that energy properly, which is my job. Helping channel it into the places it needed to go."

"Wait a minute, this brings me back to something I thought earlier." Ethan suddenly started to realize the immensity of what Death was saying. "It's just you? All the death happening in all the worlds, and it's just you doing that? Every death?"

Death nodded, smirking. "Every. Single. One."

"What about right now while you're giving me the grand tour?"

"I'm still frantically at work, doing my best to hold the fabric of the universe together before you agree to take that job off my hands."

"How?"

Death shrugged. "I am Death. I am everywhere. My reach is infinite."

Ethan turned away, looking up at the massive grass trees around him. It was so much to consider. So much to understand. It was too much for just one young man. It was too much for anyone.

"Look, I don't mean to rush your dawning epiphany, but there's more to our fungal friend over here."

Ethan looked back at Death, pointing to the shorter grass stem. "You see, this fungus here is pretty easily treatable in most cases. Pull up the grass. Treat it with a fungicide. Burn it with fire if you have to. However, here, in this place, it will be catastrophic."

Ethan wasn't done thinking about the size of the responsibility he was being asked to shoulder, but he was still listening to Death. "Why? What makes this case so damned special?"

"Easy," Death said casually, "as I explained before, it's being caused by Fusarium Blight."

"Yeah, I remember. So what?"

"So, Fusarium Blight doesn't exist in this world we currently inhabit. It is an intruder into a brand-new reality. It did not naturally evolve here. It did not float in on some breeze from the other side of the world, or even on some crashing meteorite spreading spatial funk throughout the cosmos. It is not from this particular unique plain of reality. It's as foreign as bright colors in your wardrobe."

"Bullshit. It's right there, clearly."

"Clearly, but all the same, it doesn't belong here. Sad but true. It's an interloper. A renegade biological disease that landed and infected this perfectly nice little blade of grass. They're both just doing their own thing, living in their own way, but their living like this will systematically cause the death of untold numbers of lives. Lives that would have kept on living if this tragedy of intermingling worlds had never happened. This world we're in has no reasonable means of defending itself against such a simple and treatable infestation. First the grass falls, and then the chain reaction begins. In relatively little time, on the grand scale of things, this entire world will fall. An entire planet brought down by a single fungal spore in just a few hundred years. It will be unprecedented, and I am powerless to stop it. All I can do is ensure the resulting carnage will be handled properly, which I shouldn't need to tell you is one hell of an undertaking when we're talking about life on a planetary scale."

Ethan was dumfounded. He wasn't sure if this was a trick, but the memory of that deep, crawling, unnatural feeling when he placed his hand on the grass told him it was the truth, or was as far as he could tell. "Where did the spore that caused this come from?"

"Another world. One in another reality, far beyond anywhere anyone could travel without knowledge of quantum physics so deep that they would rival God Himself in intelligence and ability."

"Yeah, ok, but that's not going to happen, so how, then? How did it get here?"

"It was simply floating through the air and slipped through a hole that shouldn't have been there. An itsy-bitsy, teeny-weeny little gap in reality. It is as innocent as the grass or Ms. Omally. A harmless passenger on the wind."

"Where did the hole come from? If you say it's so fucking rare and it shouldn't happen."

"Ah, now we're getting to the meat of the issue, aren't we? Let's just tease the reveal a bit by saying it's just one man. One person in another reality who's fucking it all up for everyone and he doesn't even realize it."

Ethan looked incredulous. Something about what Death was saying didn't add up. "Is he evil? Is he, like, just a total dick or what? Why is he doing this?" Ethan had a hard time believing anyone could cut so easily through the worlds like Death was explaining. "Didn't you say it would take someone with the strength and intelligence of God to understand how to do this?"

Death looked away, back towards the way they came and the green doorway that lay beyond. "I sure did, and thanks for listening! I know how short your attention span is, so yes, I did say that." He paused briefly, but that single moment of silence was enough to make Ethan's arms break out in goosebumps. "That is exactly what he has."

Ethan looked as if he was about to ask another question, but Death shushed him right away, pointing back to the fungus-infected grass. "Here. It's time."

Ethan watched confused as Death walked back over to the plant and looked at it deeply. "Plants die differently than animals," Death said. "Being so slow-moving in their own worlds, they can be dead and not even look like anything is wrong. Watch."

Silently, Ethan watched as Death once again touched the stem. This time, just as with the waitress, a multitude of glowing embers flew out of the grass up its entire length, radiating outward, passing through Ethan in some cases, and refilling him with that warm, pure feeling. Ethan knew what was happening now. Somewhere, somehow, deep in the core of this plant, it had just died. The thought made him terribly sad.

"There," said Death as the last sprigs of light faded away. "It's gone. Some of its core functions will continue, but eventually it will completely succumb to the fungus and wither away. Tragic, isn't it. The first casualty this world will suffer, thanks to one dick that's as powerful as God and twice as stupid, in a world full of people too full of themselves to know how dangerous they are."

Ethan was not a religious man, obviously. He had spent too many Sundays out looking for his mother or looking after whatever puddle of motherly humanity he'd found the night before Sunday's dawning hours to be bothered wandering into the pews. From his understanding of the Almighty, He wasn't exactly something that could be equaled. That said, a lot of things Ethan believed to be true were being questioned lately, so it was safe to say he was slightly more susceptible to the possibility than he'd been before leaping from a plane almost two weeks ago.

There was so much to take in, and with each moment he was sure that he was not the man for this job despite Death's insistence that opting out was not a possibility, as well as his own personal desire to actually be something special in the world. Every death everywhere, all throughout the universe? *Multiple* universes, no less? There's no way anyone could handle that. Too much is too much.

Death continued to walk on, and he unbelievably started to whistle as he went. He wasn't positive, but Ethan swore he was whistling Blondie's "Rapture." God how he hated him. So fucking casual when all of this was going on. He couldn't get it together, and it was starting to drive him mad.

They came to the door they had entered from, which had changed to a deeper, earthier shade of green. Like a dark moss. "Fuck," Death said, ceasing his whistling and losing his smile. "Are you god damned kidding me?"

Ethan looked on perplexed. "What? Explain for those of us without cosmic vision."

"Ha, there's an understatement. So it seems our way back to the glory of the everything hub world has been cut off, at least for some of us."

"You mean me, don't you." It wasn't a question. With everything that had happened, Ethan knew it had to come back to him somehow.

"Oh, look who's learning."

"I'm not learning. Shit things just happen to me."

"Ugh, so negative. And unfortunately I can't say you're wrong. I can go anywhere I like. But you, and your baffling refusal to die, are still mortal, and that means we need to travel in ways that are more sensitive to your fragile situation."

"Well, I suppose I could just kill myself to end the hassle," Ethan said jokingly, but in an instant the comically oversized gun Death had pulled out of thin air in his apartment was back in his hands.

"Perfect! Don't forget the safety. Oh, I'm kidding. My guns don't have safeties." Ethan just stared at him. "Hey, don't tease me. I've had a long day." The gun vanished again. "Alright, I'll be right back. Try not to wander off, ok?"

"I'll do my best. What's wrong with the door, anyway?"

"It's another offshoot of the otherworldly traveler's actions spreading. It's more than just grass fungus in this world, it seems. I can make *safe* ways for mortals to travel from one world to another, unlike the inter-dimensional asshole. Unfortunately his actions make bouncing around from existence to existence more dangerous. Let's say that the door here is locked from the other side until someone, ie: me, goes and fixes it. Hold tight, and don't take any wooden nickels."

Before he could explain exactly what his plan was, Death faded into nothingness, leaving Ethan all alone in the oversized grassy field.

Sweet Jesus, this was all fucked-up. Caddles and water parks and otherworldly fungus and hot waitresses who didn't speak English but were DTF just before being blown away by a massive ball of fire and turned into a collection of floating lights. Yesterday he was saying goodbye to his sister and having a few drinks with some co-workers who may or may not think of him as some kind of living god.

He sat next to one of the grass trees and waited while Death wandered off somewhere he didn't care about. Frankly he was happy for the moment of peace while he waited. That was until his stomach grumbled hungrily. Damn he was hungry. A couple shitty strawberries and some coffee was not proper existential-existence traveling fuel.

As if on cue, a new smell came to him, welcoming and subtle. It wasn't plant-like or earthy like the other smells around him. This one was warmer and more familiar. Ethan looked around, trying to find the source of the aroma. Death had told him to stay still, but he wasn't going to wander far. Besides, didn't Death proclaim that he was *everywhere*? It's not like he was going anywhere he couldn't be found.

Ethan stood and moved on, wandering down the path where the large yellow bug had come from when they first arrived. The smell got stronger as he moved, tantalizing him further. He didn't think it was possible, but he actually started becoming giddy. Maybe it was the hunger talking, but Ethan Dessier as a general rule avoided giddiness and all its trappings whenever possible, so the fact that something about that smell made him this way triggered an alarm bell. Should he be concerned?

Probably, but he was still hungry as fuck. What was that smell? It bothered him, like a word on the tip of his tongue.

He walked along until he came to another clearing. He touched other grass stems along the way, receiving a warm and peaceful feeling from each of them. The thought of all of this inheriting that gross crawling sensation made Ethan sad, but he was still certain that it wasn't anything he would be able to help with.

In the center of the small clearing the smell became stronger. It was something baked. Something bready. It smelled so good.

Ethan began walking forward again, but this time he felt restrained, as if he was being pushed back. It was an odd feeling that came from nothing that he could see. Was Death holding him back to keep him in place? Probably. He already showed himself to be untrustworthy. Why? If he could find Ethan anywhere, why put in the effort to keep him in place? Looking at the emptiness that had stopped him, he reached out with one hand and tried to get a better feeling for what it was.

His hand met the resistance, but it wasn't solid. He pushed it forward and his hand became wrapped in it, as if it was sliding into warm Jell-O. He could still see his hand, so it hadn't gone anywhere, but it was absolutely wrapped up in something.

Just go back, he told himself, *this isn't right. Death said to hang tight.* He wanted to listen to himself, but the smell, and the strange memory it triggered, drove him forward. He pushed farther.

Soon his arm was enveloped right up to his shoulder. His hand, however, no longer felt resistance and moved freely on the other side of the strange invisible disturbance. It wasn't very thick, whatever it was.

He wasn't afraid. Only curious. What could cause a sensation like this? There was only one way to find out.

He pushed his arm forward more, driving himself into the space. The enveloping feeling soon overtook his whole body, but he continued. The smell was everywhere, and he could still see everything around him perfectly, so he wasn't claustrophobic yet. The sun was shining and he could still hear the wind and the grass brushing together.

His arm up to his elbow emerged from the dense space, followed by his right leg. With one more push, his head would be through. Ethan had absolutely nothing to lose, as near as he could figure, and the thought of wandering off and making Death come find him filled him with more than a small sense of satisfaction.

So he pushed.

Chapter 10

His face emerged and at once he noticed the change in temperature. The grassy field had been warm, but the chilled wind of autumn was in the air. Now it was very hot; almost uncomfortably so. Then the rest of his senses caught up to his nose. The bright sky of the field was snuffed out as he passed through the thick air completely. It was still light, but the light was more unnatural and uninviting. Ethan blinked a number of times, adjusting his vision to view things indoors.

Wait, why was he suddenly indoors? Where the fuck was he? The sounds of the outdoors were also replaced with an abnormal clanking sound. A machine was at work, and it was nearby.

His eyes finally caught up and he readjusted his vision to see where he was. It was a hallway. The walls were white and cold. Industrial, like the corridors in the office attached to a heavy industrial factory. The light came from the standard florescent lights that lined every corporate catacomb he'd ever entered, including his own place of employment.

The air was almost stiflingly hot, and Ethan had to catch his breath for a moment in an effort to feel more comfortable and avoid being lightheaded. It was also thick, but not like what he passed through to get here. As near as he could describe it, the air here was heavy.

The smell remained, though. Warm and vaguely reminiscent of something he couldn't quite place.

He started to turn around but then hesitated, remembering the last time he had found himself in something this vaguely hall-like. Also, he still had an aversion to looking back. He blindly reached back to see if his entrance was still there, but his hand only passed through nothingness like it was supposed to.

He turned to see what was behind him, nervous ever since his previous attempt led to Ethan having all joy, light, and anything worth living for sucked from his body in a violent extraction he'd apparently never forget for as long as he lived. Eventually he caught a glimpse, and the wretched feeling of pure nothingness never came. He looked back properly, and only saw a regular hallway lined with doors and signs proclaiming *11 Days since our lost accident!* He checked a poster nearby and saw that his eyes weren't messing with him: it actually said *lost*. Was this another linguistic change for a new world, like the English that was pronounced in clicks?

He took a few steps back to see if he had just missed the way he'd come in, but it wasn't there. The Jell-O air was gone.

Fuck. he thought quietly to himself. *Death is going to kill me.* Ha. Unintentional dark humor was always the best kind of humor. He looked back down the hall the way he'd come. *Oh well, come and get me, prick.*

Ethan started walking, noting that the smell and the sounds of repeating machinery were getting stronger and louder. There was no stopping him now. He was a man on a mission. He made a quick right, followed by a left, and the hall ended in a set of swinging double doors. He grasped the handle and pushed. The door didn't move. Was it locked?

Pull, stupid, he thought to himself in Death's voice. God how he wanted to punch that smug, pale face. While thinking of how satisfying that would be, he pulled the door open and walked through.

On the other side was a huge industrial space. It was possibly the largest room Ethan could ever remember standing in. The ceiling was as tall as the blades of grass in the massive world he'd just come from. The walls were lined with windows that were grimy and blotted out all light, if there was any to blot. The outside seemed as dark as the world he'd first entered with Death on the beach, only this time there was no red sun to bathe everything in a strange radiance.

Arc lights hung from the distant ceiling, each of them swaying and bobbing in an unseen breeze. His shadows from the lights danced around him slowly as he walked into the room, entranced by the sight that was in the middle. The heat didn't bother him anymore. Only the smell and what he saw mattered now, and it all came into place as he walked.

Under a distant light sat a large machine he'd seen before at his local supermarket in the bakery section. It was some kind of industrial bread oven, with a conveyer belt passing through it to process as many baked goods as it could manage in a short period of time. The machine was in full operation, and Ethan could see the confections (it was impossible to tell exactly what they were from here, but they smelled fantastic) moving along the elevated belt and carried off into who knew where behind the machine.

In front of the machine sat an old dining room table he would know better than any other piece of shitty furniture in the whole world. It was his, from his old Chicago home. He could see it even from this far away. He kept walking.

There were two chairs around the old wooden table that may have once been fancy but now were all faded and damaged just as he'd left them. One of the chairs was missing its arm; an arm he'd tried to fix once only to have his mother throw herself into it a week later and re-break. He never tried to fix it again after that, or anything else in his house for that matter. It was too much effort for something that he didn't care about, and he was certain she'd just break again.

At the table sat his mother, looking just as she had the day he left, however, she also looked more youthful and beautiful just as he had seen her before his fall into the waterslide. It was as if she was two images at once, and his brain was having a hard time digesting which he should be focusing on.

Ethan started shaking, but he didn't stop walking. His feet echoed in the space as he moved. The sound was cavernous and empty. His mother, or the strange double-image of her, was holding her hands in front of her, watching him walk closer with a look of both drugged-out passiveness and quiet excitement. One of those looks was one he knew very well. Soon he came as close as he wanted to, and his mother stood to meet him. She didn't say a word. She only indicated he join her, gesturing to the broken chair at the opposite end of their family dinner table.

Ethan stood, shaking and angry. If this was one of Death's lessons or tricks, he sure as shit wasn't laughing. He didn't know if it was possible to murder the Grim Reaper, but if this was some elaborate show of power, Ethan was going to find out. He remained standing.

"Please," his mother said loudly, trying to speak over the machine behind her, "sit."

Ethan didn't respond. He only stood stoically. There was no way he was going to join his dead mother for a lovely chat, regardless of if she was real or not. She was a painful memory he'd worked very hard in trying to escape.

Realization dawned on the double-face of his mother. She pushed her chair back fully and walked over to a control panel on the machine. After a few presses, the machine shut down, the last of its functions echoing and rolling through the room as it did so. Satisfied, his mother returned to the table and stood at the head of it again, repeating her indication for Ethan to sit.

He remained unmoved.

"This will be so much easier if you sit. We may be here awhile."

"We won't be," Ethan said through semi-clenched teeth. "In fact, I'd like to leave right now, so if you could just show me the door..."

His mother smiled, and also frowned in depression. "There is no door," said the voice of the mother he'd hauled to the hospital rehabilitation room more than once. "There is no exit. There's nothing here but me, so I guess I'm your only way out of here."

"Bullshit," Ethan spat. "I got in here just fine, so how about you stop jerking me around and show me the way back."

His mother shook her head. "No. Not until you sit and talk."

"If you're one of Death's tricks or jokes meant to be a doorway to some fucking epiphany, I swear to God I'm gonna' see if you can die twice."

Her face, both of them, hung low in sadness. "Was I so bad?"

Ethan's face twisted. "I walked away from your hospital room, jumped on a plane and got about as far away from you as I could get without moving to another country or the hell of Southern California, so what would that tell you?"

"It tells me you gave up too early."

"Fuck you!" Ethan screamed, stepping closer to the table in anger, his face turning red. Death had alluded to this point before. After the spectral image of his mother had derailed him and sent him off to Mystic Waters, it had been creeping into his mind more and more. "You gave up on yourself! I wasn't going to let you drag me down farther into your shithole life. I knew when to cut the damn cord and that's what I fucking did!"

She sighed and proceeded to sit down. "Christ, I knew this wasn't going to be easy."

"What? What's not easy? Why the hell am I here?"

"Sit," she replied. "Sit and listen. That's all I want. It's all I've ever wanted."

His blood was still boiling. He wanted no part of this conversation at all. The pleasant smell that had led him here hung in the air and he no longer cared. He remembered it now. How could he forget?

When he was very young, shortly after his father had left, his mother used to have a weekly psychiatrist meeting every Saturday morning. Their neighbor would watch the kids while his mother would go off and get her head shrunk. The combination of depression over their father leaving, two young kids tearing up the house, and the looming threat of an alcohol problem (that would eventually lead to much more) without any help or support were too much for her, and she needed a release. In later years Ethan would reflect oddly that a single mom of two with a clear case of depression, a semi-public addiction problem, and a weekly psychiatric meeting didn't raise any red flags to anyone in their tiny circle. They were just allowed to keep on keeping on.

When the meeting was done, she would swing by the local bakery and bring home a fresh pack of blueberry muffins for them all to share. It was those very same muffins that were being churned out of the machine behind her with ruthless efficiency. Seeing one of his cherished childhood memories represented by a cold, generic machine that tied back to his mother so well was nauseating.

She still indicated the busted chair, hoping he would sit. Ethan wasn't ready to acquiesce to her in any fashion. He walked over to the chair, grasped the remaining handle firmly, and ripped it backwards as hard as he could. It splintered and ripped away from its already-tenuous grip on the chair with a pop. He tossed the broken arm off into the distance behind him, letting it rattle and clack through the fresh silence.

Not yet satisfied his point was made, he then proceeded to grab the back of the chair with an efficiency and strength he didn't think he actually possessed and slammed the chair down onto the tabletop with a crash so loud that it hurt his ears and caused his mother to flinch away while shattered pieces of the chair flew past her.

When the bouncing audible memory of the episode of unbridled anger finished its seemingly-endless trips around the room, Ethan looked back at his mother over the now badly cracked table. "I'll stand, thanks."

His mother looked on, upset, but resolute to continue the job she'd apparently given herself. "Do you know what these are?" she asked, pointing to a tray of muffins near the machine.

"They're fucking golden drops of sunshine. What the hell do you think they are?"

"I think they're a good memory. Remember before when I asked you to find one? I could have sworn this was where you'd end up. I was trying to get you to join me here so we could talk about things once I realized what Death had done and pulled you through. Where did you end up going?"

Ethan bit his lip at first, debating whether or not to answer the woman whom he loved as any son would and loathed for ruining his life. He didn't see many options other than going back into the empty hallway and seeing what was there, but this was far more self-destructive, which he had to admit was his modus operandi right now. "Mystic Waters."

The haggard face of his mother slumped back in her chair, while the more peaceful face actually remained sitting up, looking a different kind of sad. She was almost made of two different ghosts for a moment. "I hate that place."

Ethan felt like he was punched in the guts. "I don't really care what you think of it, frankly. It's my memory. Arlene and I had fun that day, and you were there. Not sure if you being there was a part of the good feelings, or if it was just good with you there by association. I don't care, either." He could feel his fingernails digging into the soft faded wood of the tabletop. The dirty lacquer from countless dirty childhood meals that was never cleaned strained against the pressure.

"I'm sorry. It's not exactly high on my list."

"Oh, let's just get it out: and why is that? You sure looked like you were having fun."

"I was high as a kite, Ethan. I only took you there because that was where my new dealer operated out of, but he got caught the next day and I needed a new one…"

"Shut the fuck up!" Ethan screamed, forcing his spectral mother back a bit. "Don't you *dare* shit all over that with your pathetic excuses and need to be saved. What the fuck is your god damned problem? You're fucking dead! You're dead and gone, and while I'm in the middle of some kind of crazy Death job interview, you pull me in here and start heaping this shit on me, even in this horrible afterlife? Not even a, 'Hey Ethan, so glad to hear you survived that terrifying plane crash'? I'm not going to offer you an ounce of forgiveness if that's what you're looking for, you self-destructive bitch! God damn, I hate you so much…"

There was silence for a moment, and Ethan couldn't fight it anymore. He could feel the dripping moisture on his cheeks and he didn't care. Where was Death to take him away and show him some world where people were actually blue space ducks and everyone voted Libertarian? Wasn't that the plan here?

He heard his mother's chair move and he looked up as she walked over to the muffin tray and brought it over to the table. "Would you like one? You used to love them. Arlene not so much."

"Yeah, no shit. Maybe that's because of her *fucking allergy to blueberries*! She'd have a few bites and break out in hives for hours."

She looked dejected, as if she'd forgotten, or worse yet, had never known. He didn't feel guilt when he looked at her face, but he sure as hell didn't feel victory either. "I'll pass, thanks. I'm hungry, but I don't want anything from you, other than for you to go away."

She held her hands up defensively. "I'm sorry, but you came here. I didn't drag you in. I tried to earlier, to help you out, but instead you left to the place where it all started to really go wrong for me; where I first sacrificed happiness for a high."

"That's crap," he spat. "I smelled those damn muffins from a whole different world! I had to see what the hell it was. I didn't dream that. Either Death is fucking with me, in which case you both better pray, or it's just you."

"No, you did it. You came here on your own. I thought I'd lost you. I waited. It's why I made the muffins."

Was she serious? How was that even possible? He needed to know the rules in this place better. "Looks like you made too many."

"The machine doesn't stop, Ethan. I started it, and it just keeps going. It stops and starts on my command, but it will keep pushing these little things out forever and ever. It's my personal version of Hell. I don't know how you got here, but I'm glad you did."

Ethan remembered Hell, or at least the Hell as Death had explained it. This wasn't nothingness. This was as real as something could be in this place. "What's wrong with muffins? You're the one who bought them."

"It was my Shrink's idea. A way of creating a connective bond between me and my family. So now I get to spend as long as it takes trying to reconnect with people who want no part of me."

"No argument there."

She sat again, but she also didn't. The aged and wicked version he knew so well tossed the muffins across the table like a Frisbee, stopping at the edge of the table right between his arms. However, the more serene and healthy-looking version of her still held the muffins in her hand and slowly walked them over to him, placing them exactly where the other version of them had landed, making them appear whole again. She then walked back, sat in the chair, and became her blended self once more.

"I'm here, alone, in a prison of my own making, Ethan. I just wanted you to know that I still think of you both, and I still love you. That's all."

He looked at her again. *Really* looked at her. Try as he might, he just didn't have a shred of strength to give her anything close to what she wanted. He wasn't happy about it necessarily, but it was what it was. "You can't leave?"

"Parts of me can, as you saw before, but no. I'm always here, tied to this place, making baked goods in a huge empty room, with no day or night. Just me, the muffins, and a boatload of bad memories."

Ethan tossed the tray back at her, but it caught the broken ridge he'd made with the chair and toppled over, spilling them across the table and on the ground. "I don't want your fucking muffins. I don't want your bad memories. I just want you to go away."

Her soft face turned red, and her drugged one got angry. "I did what I could," she said in a voice that was both sad and angry. "I'm sorry it wasn't good enough for you." The soft voice spoke the words as a genuine apology, but the angry one spit it out with malice and sarcasm.

It still didn't get to him like she might have hoped it would. Whatever powers of persuasion she may have thought she possessed over him, or thought she could invoke with pity, never materialized. "You're my mother," he said at last, fighting back tears while swearing he wouldn't ever shed another one for this woman, "you fucking should be sorry."

Without another word, he turned to leave. He didn't care if he had to smash the bricks and mortar of this spectral building down with his bare hands; he was not going to spend another minute in this room with someone he loathed so much.

He had almost reached the double-door out to the strange hallway when his mother called out his name, both with ferocity and kindness in equal measure. Foolishly, although he didn't turn around, he did stop.

"Death is right," she continued, "you are the strongest one for the job. Good luck!"

He exited into the hall as quick as he reasonably could without looking like he was trying to run away from something that scared him and went back to the spot where he had entered.

Thankfully, when he reached out this time, he felt that same resistance. Knowing what to expect, he shoved his way through like a linebacker, and emerged into the sun and minty freshness that awaited him on the other side.

Chapter 11

He lied. He lied to himself. He knew it at once as he emerged in the greenery of the oversized field. He lied, and he was furious with himself about it. He said he wouldn't do it, but he did, and he couldn't stop it.

He cried. He cried harder and with more force than he could ever remember. He sobbed like a small child until his voice started to crack and his diaphragm hurt in the depths of his guts. His inhaling stuttered and his nose began to run, but he was powerless to stop it.

He didn't see Death anywhere, but that didn't mean he wasn't watching. He hated the thought of giving him the smug satisfaction of seeing him like this, but at least he had gotten away from his mother before he broke. Muffins? Seriously? She was apparently in her own personal Hell and it was nothing but empty space and muffins? Of everything he'd seen so far today, this was the one that made the least amount of sense.

He was doubled over on the ground for a number of minutes trying to compose himself, eager to make the moment pass. *I need to stop*, he thought, over and over again. *I need to keep control*.

He took deep breaths, just as he had at the funeral. Deep, long breaths that filled his nose and lungs with the sweetness and beauty of the space he inhabited. He hadn't cried for her then, so why the fuck was he doing it now?

Not in the plane crash. Not when his sister had broken down in his arms. Why now?

Soon, when his body ached and his eyes hurt, he stopped. The moment passing, but never the memory. He knew he looked like shit. He remembered looking in the mirror in the hospital just before Death's second appearance, amused at how bad he looked. He likely wasn't any better now, and his face was certainly a lot more red and puffy.

Ethan Dessier was blessed with that tremendous ability to pick himself up and soldier on, but God knows where he got it from. It had apparently saved his life in the *Puget Plunge (*patent under review), and it forced him now to get up, try his almighty damndest to put that brave, disassociated face back on, and wander back towards the mossy-colored door that had brought him here to await Death's return.

He walked on in silence, only passively noting the activity around him. Insects milled and buzzed around, filling the air with life. Even staring at the ground as he traveled, Ethan could feel them moving. Everything here was alive, and the glory of that life continued to fill him in ways he both detested and enjoyed. This was a beautiful place. It was so tiny, in the grand scheme of things, but there was so much going on. So much to enjoy.

In his recovery, he remembered the fungus. It was spreading and was going to kill everything around him that was filling him with light and helping the pain of crying so hard go away, all because of some dipshit in another reality. The anger at his encounter with his mother transferred itself to this unseen ultra-powerful being in another world that was causing shit like this to happen.

He didn't know who this fucker was. If Death was to be believed (which was still questionable at this point) there was another world out there where humans had god-like superhero powers, and one of them was really disturbing the shit. After all he'd seen during this fucked-up day, was that really so unbelievable? Wasn't he actually the height of a bug in some strange distant dimension right now? No matter how much he doubted everything, or how much he believed was true, he knew beyond any doubt the gross, digging, infesting feeling he had when he touched that blade of grass was both real and horrible. He felt the life draining away, and watched as the light of life poured out and into the nothingness.

He could feel that same life all around him now. Strong. Peaceful. It was a beacon against the cold emptiness in the place at the back of the path on the beach. Like a light that cut through the darkness. If one sprig of grass could make him feel so full of life, and so hurt at its death, then the thought of the same thing happening to the entire world around him made him feel sick.

So this cross-dimensional Superman motherfucker was going to end this and others like it all throughout the cosmos? Jeez, no matter what reality they lived in, humans were always assholes. Intentional deaths or not, he was damn sure he wasn't about to let something so beautiful die.

It was an uncharacteristically sentimental thought for him to have, but every time he thought he was crazy, he remembered the smell of blueberry muffins. His anger at his encounter with his mother still bubbled, but he smiled slightly at the thought that the only way to counter her brand of chaos was not to destroy something in a rage, but actually trying to preserve something wonderful. He couldn't go back to take his fury out on his mother for playing with his emotions and attempting to destroy the memory of what was the greatest, happiest day he'd ever had, but he could damn sure do something about this, couldn't he?

Yes, he could. He wasn't Death. At least, not yet (decision still pending), so that meant he didn't have to play by Death's rules. He couldn't bend realities and influence nature itself, but he could damn sure do what humans did best, regardless of space, time, or supernatural whatnots.

He could be an asshole.

He found the door, which remained closed and dark. He even tested it to make sure it wasn't some trick, but the massive door remained locked. Good. That gave him time.

He went back to the clearing with the grass sprouts, where the first of what was apparently going to be a global-scale number of deaths had just occurred. He wasn't even sure he trusted Death regarding what was about to happen to this place. Death was either telling the truth and something needed to be done, or he was lying for kicks or some bullshit educational purpose and he needed to be shown that Ethan Dessier may be a moping millennial asshole, but he wasn't going to be anyone's puppet.

Thankfully, the sun was still out. He placed his hand on the grass stem that he'd witnessed the death of and wasn't surprised to find that the life of the plant was gone. Only the more disturbing, writhing life of the fungus from another dimension remained, clawing its way up from deep inside.

He had the idea almost immediately. He walked into the clearing not sure what to do, but now that he was standing here, the answer was obvious. Death had said it himself. He had provided the solution to the problem. Ethan really hoped it wasn't intentional. He wanted this action to be his own.

He removed his glasses from his pocket and slid them out of their cloth case. He remembered getting these. He was having trouble in school, and although that was primarily due to the systematic destruction of his family life, he was also having trouble seeing things clearly. His mother, in the middle of a *deny deny deny* episode, immediately took him to get glasses after convincing herself that improper vision was the primary reason for his slipping, which in the end only marginally improved his life and did nothing at all for his grades. Still, he needed them now, no doubt about it. He was thankful he was able to come up with a solution so easily. Unsurprisingly, being a self-destructive ass came quite naturally to him.

Ethan held them up to make sure they were clear, and then found a collection of fibrous pieces hanging off of the dead stalk that were in the sun. He held his glasses over them, trying desperately to focus the sunlight like a child trying to roast ants. It wasn't as easy as he hoped it would be. Magnifying glasses were so simple to do this with, but prescription glasses took a measure of finesse. Soon, after a number of minutes of trying and readjusting, the smoke started. He was never outdoorsy or particularly inclined to know any survivalist techniques, but he'd seen enough TV and movies to get the gist. He stopped with the glasses and started to lightly blow on the smoldering spot he'd created. As if by a Divine combination of luck and magic, the small fire started just as he planned.

When it goes unchecked and has enough fuel to do what it does best, fire is particularly easy to spread. That was the case here as all the fibers that line the grass in every direction, that would normally be microscopic if he was his regular size, were set alight. Ethan stepped back as the fire began to engulf the little grove of grass, eventually stretching all the way up to their tops. The wind gusted at those heights, and soon it was spreading to other plants in the area. It made Ethan feel queasy, but also invigorated. He could feel the life leaving these plants, though he couldn't see the glowing balls as they died. He must need Death for that.

As if on cue, Death reappeared by the door as Ethan walked back. Ethan wasn't sure if he'd ever seen anyone so enraged in all his life, and he was a man who had seen a middle-aged woman tear a house apart looking for just one more pill, slicing open stuffed animals and destroying a little girl's dollhouse.

Death was changed. Gone were the Crocs and board shorts. Now there were thick black work jeans, a black tank top that clearly exposed the tattoo on his arm, (*I'm sorry, is that an…?*) and heavy black hiking boots. It was the first time Ethan could remember him wearing an outfit that actually seemed to go together. Every piece was still the same light-absorbing black. "What the fuck do you think you're doing?!?!" Death screamed, running off towards the clearing where it had all started. Ethan ran after him, but not before noticing that the door had changed back to the more lively green it had been the first time he'd come through it.

Death stopped before getting too close to the growing inferno, which was now pumping grey smoke into the air. Ethan came up behind him with a smile of smug satisfaction on his face. This was just what he was looking to accomplish. Death reeled on him, practically foaming at the mouth. "What the fuck is wrong with you? We don't kill anything!"

"No, *you* don't kill anything. You're the one bound by some bullshit intergalactic Hippocratic oath. I'm just a mortal punk kid with a self-destructive streak. You should really be more careful about who you drag with you on multidimensional excursions to the afterlife."

Ethan was certain he'd never seen anyone or anything so angry as the man standing before him. He swore he could feel red rage pouring out of Death like heat from a bonfire. "You've doomed an entire ecosystem! Every plant, insect, and small animal within miles is going to go up in smoke!"

"And fungus," Ethan added, smirking like he remembered the punchline to joke that no one else knew. "Don't forget all the fungus."

Rage radiated off of Death as he looked back at the ever-growing fire. "What the fuck do you mean fun…" It hit him, and at once Ethan could tell that this wasn't some elaborate trick by Death. Death, the powerful and eternal entity, actually didn't get it, and the realization just dawned on him. "You… You torched an entire field, sacrificing countless lives, just to eradicate the fungus?"

"Yep," said Ethan with a smile, "that's exactly what I did."

"Jesus suffering fuck, kid. Your self-destructive tendencies, although sometimes delightfully amusing, don't bring a lot of value to the table."

"Don't they? Was I successful? Is it dead?"

Death looked livid, but still reached out with his hands, almost as if he was a set of rabbit ears on an old TV, trying to pick up one specific signal. When he opened his eyes, Ethan knew the answer before Death spoke. "It's dead."

Ethan nodded smugly. "Fucking right it is. Poof. Problem solved. Planet saved. Can we go now?" He started to go back to the door, eager to see if he was right and it could be opened. "Frankly, for a guy who can cause massive destruction like earthquakes and 9/11 and Washington State plane crashes, I would have thought you could have come up with that yourself."

Death just stood flabbergasted. The fire raged on, and after a few moments of contemplation, he finally decided to join Ethan by the door. Ethan was feeling particularly accomplished, though he wasn't sure he had any right to. The fire grew, more lives were lost, and his anger at his mother was far from gone. Still, he at least felt like he'd *done* something. Shifted the paradigm. Rocked the boat. Made a mark on the world that wouldn't be there without him. He actually had to admit that it was pretty fucking satisfying. Better than a day at work fetching coffee for corporate real estate douchebags.

Death looked lost. "You didn't make any preparations, though. Nothing to help maintain the balance like Death is supposed to. You didn't accomplish anything here other than destroying something beautiful."

"Something, that according to you, was going to be destroyed anyway. Seems like a pretty clear case of 'the needs of the many outweigh the needs of the few.'"

"Dear fucking God, if this is another *Star Trek* moment in our relationship, I swear to all that is holy…"

"Can you fix this?" Ethan interjected.

"What do you mean?"

"You keep going on about maintaining the balance, making sure the essence of all the lives you take every moment of every day are spread around the galactic teeter-totter so god damned perfectly, so, can. You. Fix. This?"

"Of course I can, but it's not the way it's supposed to be. The balance is being disrupted even now, with all this unnatural and unexpected death."

"Is it better than a whole planet?"

Death sneered. "Don't think you're so fucking smart, kid. You are dancing on the edge of my tolerance and you have two left feet."

Death never answered the question directly, but Ethan could tell it was a *yes*. "Alright, so this ass from some far-off place is fucking with things, but maybe burning the forest down is what you need."

"I'm sorry, are you dipping into *Dark Night* territory? Are you just a rolling pile of clichés?"

"Just think about it. Why me? What's so special about me? I'm a depressed twenty-something with no direction and a strange refusal to die."

The fire approached them, and although Ethan was pretty certain that no harm would come to them, Death still looked at it with trepidation before looking back at Ethan. "I need you because you are who the universe told me to track down. You are the Deathmore we need for the problem. I need a Chaotic Good to defeat a Lawful Evil."

"I never played Dungeons and Dragons."

"Yeah, says the guy who caught the reference. Look, I don't get it either, but Death doesn't make mistakes."

"You're so sure?"

"Positive as the nipple of a battery."

"So," Ethan motioned to the door, "show me." Death looked at him perplexed. "You say you're constantly shuffling the balance of the universe back and forth, even now during our witty banter. Show me."

"You have no idea what you're asking. It's so far beyond you, Ethan."

"Prove it. Blow my mind. What is this fuss all about? I want to know. Can't take a job if I don't know all the responsibilities that go with it, can I?"

Death smirked. "Alright. Challenge accepted." He grasped the door handle. "Your mental health is criminally unprepared for what I'm going to do to you," he pulled, and the door opened to a world Ethan couldn't begin to recognize, "but it will be funny as hell." With a surprising amount of strength and dexterity, Death grasped Ethan's arm and yanked him through the door by force.

Ethan was so shocked by the sudden aggressiveness of Death that he could barely register the other sensations happening to his body as he moved. At first he felt like he was falling, similar to the first encounter with his mother, but that wasn't accurate. His stomach wasn't giving any indication of motion. It was closer to say he was weightless.

He tried to focus his eyes on all the things he was seeing, but it was impossible. An image wrapped all around him, and it was too difficult to focus on. He quickly put his glasses on to see if it helped, but he was certain it only made things worse.

It appeared that he was floating in a spherical rainbow, as if someone had taken one of those wavy color patterns on his computer and encompassed him with it, and his eyes and brain couldn't determine if it was inches from his face or a million miles away. It easily could have been both, as well as all points in between. Was he floating inside it? Was it even three dimensional?

He was getting dizzy, but he had nowhere to fall. He couldn't hear anything. It was pure, disorientating silence. There was nothing to indicate if he was up or down or spinning in circles. It was like a sensory deprivation chamber for everything but his vision, and that was completely overloaded.

"Crazy, isn't it?" said a voice just below a whisper in the back of his head. "I've been here before and it still blows my feeble mind. I can't imagine what it's like for you right now. I'd guess it's probably like holding a hundred-watt bulb behind your eyes or something."

"Where… where am I?" Ethan asked. Or at least, he thought he did. The voice he heard came strictly through his head, although he was certain he had said it out loud. He remembered moving his mouth to do it. Or did he? He was hazy now. The sensations he was feeling made it difficult to remember or experience anything clearly.

"You," the voice continued, "are in the best possible representation I can give a human mind for the basic *everything* I am trying to save. A visual collection of existence. An actual snapshot of all creation, that I haven't dumbed down into a pleasant galactic walk."

"It's just a giant rainbow," Ethan's voice vibrated again. It was as if he was speaking though the bones in his head and not into the air in front of his face.

"Well that's a tragic oversimplification of what you're currently witness to, but oh well. It is what it is.

"You see, this is everything, in an image of pure light. In a moment I'll add to your sensations, but for now let's just stick with hitting you in the eyeballs. Your voice won't carry. Your fingertips will feel nothing. Your farts won't stink. Just a pure image of light, broken into all of its base components. A trillion times more colors than your little brain could ever hope to process, and a trillion times more than even that are out there. This is what happens when human eyes see things they were never meant to comprehend. Becoming Death will allow you to see what I see, without frying a circuit you may need to survive."

"I… I don't like it. I feel lost in space, and claustrophobic and tied up, all at the same time."

Even in all of this majesty, the snark could be heard in Death's voice. "Well, I'm sure some scientist or psychologist somewhere would give two shits about what you're experiencing right now, but I'm no scientist. I'm just a humble squirrel. Now, listen up, because I'm kinda running out of time and I hate repeating myself.

"The light, the love, the energy that comes from all death; the essence of what a living thing is, comes here when it's done being shackled by whatever form it was born into or collected by. Death's role is to guide it to this place and find its proper location in this nigh-infinite spectrum. What color were those soft lights that came from the woman and the grass?"

"They were white," Ethan said, trying not to lose his mind. For some reason he felt like an in-utero fetus, floating with no real up or down. His ears could hear both perfect silence and every sound ever imagined, and he actually felt as if he could *see* both. It was like he was on the acid trip to end all acid trips, even though he'd never once touched that shit. He used his own voice to try and keep himself centered. "They were all white."

"Racist. Just kidding; you're correct, and white is made up of every color, and so many more you think you know but you don't. Light beyond the spectrums you can read. Once that pure essence of life comes here, it fractures and finds its proper place in the balance of life. In the great scale of everything.

"But it's not a perfect system. Anomalies that crept up in these endless chains over time started to deflect these essences to places they shouldn't have been. Everything is made of this essence, and if it breaks apart and misses its place in the universes, then it throws things out of whack. So, when it started to become too much for a perfect system to take, necessity created a being to see this spectrum much the way you are seeing it now, and make sure everything landed where it's supposed to. Hence, Death, or the abstract concept that humans would come to call 'Death', was created; to be there at the moment of release, and guide the light home."

"Abstract… concept?"

"Of course. You don't think *Death* is an actual thing, do you? A dark man who claims souls at the moment of the end of their lives? Please. You call me Death, hell, I call me that too, but I'm just a manifestation of this everythingness. I have been around since before something was alive enough to die, and die enough to be alive."

"I don't get it…" Ethan felt as if he was losing consciousness. "We're all light?"

"In this oversimplified interpretation, yes. Light in an infinite array of colors, and it's my job to help you find your place when the pieces that are within you, within all life, and even within things like the rocks, stars, asteroids, things you don't think are alive as you understand it, leave you. It's all just a massive part of this. Endless worlds. Endless amounts of this you see before you. From reds so deep you'd swear it was empty, to violets so heightened that even I have a hard time grasping it, and I'm the caretaker of this place. It's so much for your mind, and I'm just explaining it in as rudimentary a way as I think I can pull off without turning you into a vegetable, just remember that."

"G…Gee… Thanks… 'Preciate it."

"My God. A sense of humor even in the midst of all creation. Maybe you really are the right one for the job."

"I want out."

"Oh, I bet you do, but not before the best part. Remember I said I'd add to your sensations? Well, let's not wait anymore…"

"No… No more… I can't…"

"You're right, you can't, but you're going to anyway. A mind as young and unformed as yours can't possibly understand, but it needs to be done. Remember that warm, squishy feeling you get from the things you found on our journeys? The light that filled your soul when the nothingness took it away?"

"Y…yes…" Ethan was fading. He was going to pass out. He could feel it coming.

"Well, here's an unrestricted, unfiltered dose. Straight from the tap, boss."

It was on him in an instant, filling him with glory, warmth, and light. He was no longer Ethan Dessier. He was no longer anything recognizable as human. He was nothing but a vessel for the purity. It was amazing. It was as if he was connected to everything all at once.

There was more, though, and as much as his mind demanded to experience this moment for the rest of eternity, an unknown switch in his head flipped, and he knew what else was coming. His thirst for this filling feeling was coupled with his dread.

"I serve the balance, Ethan," Death's voice said, coming from everywhere at once, reaching into every fiber of his existence. "Without the balance, the scales will collapse, and the antithesis of this feeling you are now utterly blessed with will consume everything. They are the forces forever at war, and the balance is so tenuous."

"Nnnn…nnnn…nnoooo…."

"Oh, sunshine. You don't have a choice. Every drink of the Everything comes with a Nothing chaser."

The memory forced itself in, and then, just as he was filled with the power of everything, he was simultaneously hit with the rot of the nothingness from the depths of the tunnel until the two forces were at loggerheads inside his very being fighting for control. He was only a witness on the sidelines. A spectator in his own body as gods battled to an epic standstill inside the mind and soul of an unprepared and unwilling human asshole.

There were no words anymore. There was no escape. There was only the war inside him.

And then, there was only blackness.

Chapter 12

His head hurt as if he was hungover, and considering the experience that had put him in this state, maybe he was? Was this drugs? Is this what his mother had been reaching out for all that time? Christ, maybe he was too hard on her.

At first fearful of what he may see, Ethan opened his eyes. The feeling inside him of titans clashing was gone, but that didn't make him feel any better since the memory remained. He didn't *think* he was going to see that glorious and terrifying barrage of light and color, but he didn't really know anything anymore. He opened his eyes, and was instantly relieved, confused, and upset.

A hospital. He was in a hospital bed. Again. Fucking hell...

He sat up gingerly; his head aching just like it had the day he woke up from the crash...

...Oh hell... please God tell me that wasn't all a dre...

"Morning, sport. How's the head?" Death sat smiling happily in a chair in the corner with his legs crossed and arms folded. He was wearing the same outfit as before, only he'd added an ill-fitting motorcycle jacket over it that was two sizes too large. The sleeves hung down past his hands. "They wanted to give you some sorta drug to ease the pain, but I advised them off of it. I didn't get deep into your personal history or anything, but I..."

"What happened?"

Death stopped smiling. "You passed out. A perfectly human response to what I did to you, I suppose. I'd say you did a great job putting up with that much stimulation for as long as you did.

"Anyway, I don't have a lot of hands-on skill when it comes to saving people. Just the opposite, actually, so I thought I'd bring you back to this hospital you love so much."

It was true. This was the UW Med Center alright. How fitting. "So it wasn't all some crazy dream. Thank God…"

"A dream? Everything you've witnessed and you have the nerve to say that? We're going to break through that wall of clichés you have built up one day. No, Ethan, no dream. Far from it. Here, take a look outside." Death got up and walked over to the window, pulling back the curtains. Ethan could see exactly what he was referring to.

"The sky is green!"

"Yep, and the trees are red, and all humans talk in a strange honking language they share all around the world, which I don't need to tell you is terribly conven-ient. I call this 'Circus World'. Because everybody sounds like clowns! Get it!"

"Yeah, I get it. Very clever. How long was I out?"

Death frowned slightly. "Two days. Safe to say you're late for work."

"What do you mean? This isn't my world."

"No, but time marches on. It is the constant. The true first dimension, not the fourth like your physicists think. Time is an arrow through all worlds, and it can't be stopped. I can slow it down and even see where it's going sometimes, but I can't take it back or make it go someplace it's not supposed to go. Two days here is two days everywhere. Add in the majority of the first day you already spent with me, and you're actually three days behind. I had really hoped it was all going to be done in just that one day, but your little escapade of willful defiance with that fire changed the plan. Needless to say, we're really out of time now. I was never meant to be Death for as long as I have been. I was supposed to have a day, maybe two tops."

Ethan had a defeated, smug grin. "Sorry, but I'm not actually sorry. It's just something we say, right?" They both smirked.

"Look, I think I've done everything I can to convince you of what needs to be done, and I'm running out of ideas. Tell me what you think. Tell me where we go from here." Death looked legitimately concerned.

"I think… Arlene is going to kill me."

Death moped slightly. "Probably. Not a bad way to go, actually, since that's the end goal to this adventure. Murdered by someone you love. Quite possibly the *only* one. It seems fitting."

Ethan stood, fighting the protests of his head. "Where are my clothes?"

Death held his hands out and they appeared instantly. So did his oversized handgun. "Thanks." Ethan took the clothes with one hand and the gun with the other. It was as light as a feather despite the size.

Death looked at him apprehensively and also somewhat expectantly; as if a long journey was about to come to an end. Ethan put the clothes back on the bed and looked at the gun. "This is real? This isn't some magic gun that shoots lollipops and is only a representation of a point you're trying to prove?"

Death nodded. "Real as the sun and stars, kid."

Ethan looked at it, his face reserved to some deep-seeded conclusion.

"It's the right thing, Ethan. I'm sure you see that now. Your strength is what's needed. Your ability to defy the natural order and stand against this far-off problem. I see it now. I know the reason it needs to be you. I'm sure you do, too."

Ethan nodded, but it didn't make what he was about to do any easier. "I know. An enemy that huge needs a will just as strong as his. You think that's me."

"I don't *think*. I've seen that it's true. You won't just accept what hand you've been dealt. You may try to fight out of it. You may even have hope that there's a better way, but in the end, when faced with unimaginable odds, instead of giving up, you'll stack the deck. That's what we need."

"We?"

"Everyone. Everything. Myself included. When I'm gone and you take over, I'm still a part of this system of infinite glory, right? If the balance shifts that badly, we all go down with this ship, and that nothingness will take over. No one, nothing is spared. The balance will fall, and everything will simply become nothing."

"How?"

Even drifting in this miasma of everything, Ethan could see Death smirk at him. It was a look that cut through even the most glorious of mind trips. "Ooo, exposition time again, eh? I'll be quick: it's a balanced system, as you're no doubt sick of me saying. The two sides are constantly at war. The nothing meets the something. The unstoppable force meets the immovable object, and the two cancel each other out and burst into a simultaneous state of neutrality. Great for Switzerland, only ok for us. The more powerful an entity, the more pure, then the more of that light is created inside them or absorbed from the natural universe. So when a god dies, or death happens on such a large scale like, oh I don't know, burning down a huge grassland, too much of the light escapes at once to balance properly. So this Enemy of the State out there causing all these imbalances is a problem I can't handle. Not right now. Maybe never. The imbalances cause too much light to be absorbed and distributed incorrectly, and the nothing starts to win. It's like a seesaw if you start to ever so slightly unbalance one side. Eventually it topples, and it all comes crashing down."

"Isn't it your job, or I guess *my* job, to stop that? Put everything in its place?"

"Ah, nice to see you coming around. Do you know what happens when you get too much of something at once? It overflows. Even as all-powerful as I am, sometimes I can't keep up."

"Death is fallible?"

"Watch it, shithead. I'm saying even the great care-taker of the universe can only do so much and move so fast. Mankind was never made to hold the kind of power he and those like him possess."

"There are *more*?"

"Yes, look, they're not important to this story. Only he is, and he doesn't even know the trouble he's causing. Frankly we're spending too much time focusing on him. Let's get back to the gun at hand, because he's getting closer and closer to upsetting things past a point you can reasonably fix."

Yeah. The gun. The way out, into a world where that Everything and Nothing remained at war within Ethan for as long as he holds the title of Death. Not a welcoming prospect. Still, he knew what he had to do. He knew it the moment he met his mother and started the fire. It was a hard choice, and one that many wouldn't (or couldn't) make in his position when faced with so much evidence to the contrary. They would give up and accept the end that seemed unstoppable. His will was the key. It would have to carry him through.

Arlene was going to kill him...

He held the gun in his hand, and Death went noticea-bly silent as closed his eyes, almost expectantly. *Oh well*, thought Ethan, *time to dance*.

He lifted his arm, pointed the barrel, and pulled the trigger.

Chapter 13

The smile on Death's face, as if being released from a hard day at a long job, was erased instantly with the sound of shattering glass. Ethan took no small amount of satisfaction in watching Death go from elation to confusion to rage all at one time.

The bewilderment on Death's face continued as Ethan casually and confidently held his eyes and strolled over to the window. With a smooth flick of his wrist, he tossed the weapon out the hole he'd made, grinning like a pig in shit as he did so. "Oh fuck, I hope no one finds that. Take care of it, would you please? I'd hate for anyone to die unnecessarily." Death looked at Ethan flabbergasted while the young man turned and started to get dressed.

Death was beside himself in fury, confusion, and total loss. "What…? Why…? What the fuck did you just do?!"

Ethan started pulling his underwear on, taking off his robe in the process. "I just threw your stupid gun out the window, Death. I was sick of the sight of it."

"What is wrong with you?" Death spit at him, his pale face turning a shade of red generally reserved for tomatoes, fire engines, and massive suns on other plains of existence. "Don't you get it? What more do I need to do to convince you? You've felt that nothingness! You know how horrible it is, and yet you still refuse to follow along!

We're all going to get wiped from reality in a way so horrible it makes *me* scared, and I'm fucking *Death*!"

"I need you to tell me why my mother is in Hell," Ethan said coolly while finishing getting dressed as best he could while playing the most dangerous game of brinksmanship that had likely ever been played. "I need you to explain why she's apparently trapped in some prison of her own making, split between the mom I know and the mom I wish she was, forever making fucking blueberry muffins to atone for some sin she can't escape! Did you do that to her? Did someone else? Why! And I need you to tell me quick before we get rushed by a frantic hospital staff that will want to know why a gun just went off in here."

Death sized up Ethan at once, looked at the door quickly as the handle was being turned, and reached out and grabbed Ethan by the collar of his T-shirt. He lifted Ethan off the ground and held him inches from his face. Ethan could almost smell the anger coming off of him, but he held firm. He wasn't going to get manipulated. Not by his mother. Not by Death. Not by anyone.

A rush of doctors and hospital staff ran into the room and saw Death, which to them was just a pale middle-aged man, lifting their mysterious young man in the air in a very non-complimentary way. A shattered window blew a breeze all around them, and they started shouting at the two of them.

Of course to Ethan, it just sounded like comical honking. "Oh. My. God," he said with a wry smile. "That is fucking hilarious."

With a scream so primal Ethan thought it would shatter his eardrums, Ethan watched as Death turned and tossed him like a ragdoll, throwing him across the room and right at the far wall from the bed. Ethan didn't even flinch. He was old hat at this now. He hit the wall, and then simply fell through it as if it was made of Jell-O.

Pushing through such a space was a familiar feeling to Ethan, however, that didn't change the strangeness he felt as he traveled into the open air on the other side. It was then he realized his mistake.

By his own admission, Death couldn't kill him, but he could likely hurt him really badly. Ethan briefly caught a glimpse of the fluorescent-lit ceiling of the hospital giving way to the star-dotted blackness of space. And then, much like a person walking down a hallway with their eyes closed can feel the walls and doors, he could feel the ground rushing at him without actually seeing it. The sudden impact rocked Ethan, spinning his body around and dragging it across the ground that was certainly not soft like the wall of thick air had been. It felt like coarse cement, ripping and scratching at him as he slid like a rider tossed from a motorbike. He wouldn't have thought anyone could throw a fully-grown man that hard, but then Death was no regular person, was he?

Ethan stopped, his head screaming at what had just happened, and his body was slowly lighting on fire from the number of scratches he'd just endured. Still, he was alive. He looked around, though a part of him already knew where he was.

Mystic fucking Waters.

He was in the wave pool, which had been drained just like all of the others in this fantasy world. The rips and scratches he suffered came from the textured cement bottom of the pool.

Ethan stood up. He was pretty sure he sprained something in his right ankle, but that wasn't about to stop him. He looked around, and sure enough he was back in the bizarre alternate space-world his mother had brought him to (unintentionally). The red sun burned bright, and the planets kept rotating in the distance while the echoes died away and the waterslides fell silent. The deep feeling of peace and fulfillment came back to him, and he was careful not to let his mind trigger the conflicting nothingness.

Death emerged from the space in front of him, likely where he'd come through. He stepped with purpose and determination. Ethan was worried, but still not outright afraid. Not yet, anyway. It was certainly possible he'd gone too far. He had no idea how Death was going to react.

Death looked at the damage he'd done to Ethan with smug satisfaction. "Guess you should have worn a motorcycle jacket, ass," he snarled, indicating his own oversized coat. Ethan simply stood defiantly. "You are just one big fucking joke," Death said angrily while holding his ground a number of steps away from Ethan. The words fell dead in the air. Everything was still. "So I'm going to make this as plainly serious as I can: You're going to be fucking Death, because Death says so, and that's all the reason you god damned need."

"You look like you're getting angry again. I thought we were past that."

Death's blood boiled, but he didn't move. "We were never past it. I'm just fantastic at hiding it. Now, here's what's going to happen…"

"Stop." Ethan held his hand out. Did he actually just *shush* Death? "You don't get to continue. You are completely powerless here, so no matter what you say or do, I fucking win. You gotta play my way, or this game is over."

Death was practically foaming now, spitting out every word with venom. "It's not a fucking game! God damn it, Ethan! Take this shit seriously! Crushing nothingness! The end of everything! All because some petulant little shit refuses to die for the greater good, right after burning down millions of lives for that very same reason!"

"Petulant? Ouch, you wound me, but still, nothing here has changed." Death glared at him, looking for him to continue and explain himself. "My mother. Go. Did you take me to her? Was that all a plan of yours? Is she really trapped there forever?"

Death just stood firm, took a deep breath, and started. "I put her there." Ethan was about to shout at him, but Death silenced him with a hand wave of his own. "I do that for all the troubled souls that can't let go just yet. The ones too weak to live but too scared to die. How do you know about her, anyway?"

Ethan cocked an unsure eye at Death. "You really don't know? No bullshit? No more of your stupid machinations?" Death shook his head. Ethan had no choice but to believe him. "Let's just say I ran into her. Keep talking."

"Fine. What you think you saw wasn't real. It was a visual representation of a conflicted life force trying to balance their own energy. Eventually they always make it out and get to where they're supposed to go, but it takes time, which as I've said, doesn't stop."

"It's fucking purgatory? A holding tank for the dead?"

"Yeah, basically. I wish I could spin it another way, but even in the world of death that I've shown you, there's so many shades of grey. I know you'll get it when you take over, and you will take over, but for your tiny little mind right now, you can see it that way all you want."

"That seems like a pretty fucked-up thing to do to someone."

"Ha. They do it to themselves. And the day I take job advice from you is the day I hang up my robe and scythe."

"Do you really have those?"

"God you're an idiot," Death whispered as an aside. "No! Obviously I don't. I already told you what *death* was, and it's not some creepy Slenderman in a robe!"

"Well, this all fucking sucks for you then, doesn't it? I'm not super-keen on taking on a role where I have to willfully leave my mother in her own personal Hell, let alone cast others into that same place."

"They get out. They always get out. They've never *not* gotten out! But they need time, which I'm happy to give them. Frankly, it's a real time-saver.

Death seemed to be cooling down from the hospital incident, looking to defuse the situation as best he could. "Ethan, your mother fucked up. She was trapped in her own little Hell long before that last OD took her life. She's just working it out now, in her own way. I told you she wanted to die, but she wasn't ready for what death actually was. Her and millions more like her. You can accept death easily, and even be *ready* to die, but you may not be able to accept what comes after. It's not an uncommon malady."

"No shit. Seems a pretty clear description right now, doesn't it."

"Yeah, I suppose so."

"How did I get there? How did I find her?"

Death sighed. "Likely because you wanted to. Or some part of you did. Couple that with her desire to be found, and poof, there you go. You're not Death yet, but you are a Deathmore. A real, living one in a place where that has never happened. The infallible cosmic Everything granted you and all other Deathmores a general pass to do these kinds of things, but you're the first one to ever actually do it since all the others just fucking *died*! It's like a backstage pass to the afterlife, where you get to hang out with the band but not actually put on the show. Not to mention your iron fucking will to live for some god damned reason. It's not too far a stretch to say it happened because you wanted it to, but for simplicity let's just say it was crazy Death magic and move the fuck on."

Silence for a moment. The impasse between them was so tangible they could both taste it. Death spoke first.

163

"Ethan, you need to let it go. These desires to hang on for no reason other than you think you have to, it's done. Your mother will find her place. They always do. Your sister will live a long full life, so long as nothing overly-stupid happens to her. You just need to get past this. You need to forget about your mother's situation, and this stupid water park, and that damn plane crash…"

"Hey, I'd love nothing more than to forget, but something like a plane crash is hard to ignore."

"Oh c'mon. Like Bob Seger said: turn the page."

"I thought that was Metallica?"

Another near-audible eyeroll from Death. "Ugh. Fucking millennials."

They both looked at each other and smiled after a moment. It cut through the air nicely, and Ethan was more comfortable now. "Will Arlene really be ok?"

Death nodded. "I can't predict the actions of others, or the willfulness of nature, but if she carries on like she is now, she'll be more than fine. Also, you know you can visit her, right? I mean, I'm here with you, but I'm also everywhere else doing my fucking job. I'm not saying you need to cut each other from your lives."

Huh. Death was right. Still, he knew it wasn't that easy. He didn't know why he knew it, but he just did. It wasn't an outside voice telling him so; it was his own. A strong voice. One he believed. Just about the only voice he trusted.

Ethan weighed the possibilities and eventually knew what he had to do. He knew the answer stronger now than when he dragged his strung-out mother to the hospital, or while holding his crying sister all those nights that their mom was on a rage outside the door. He knew it when he first felt that damned plane lurch forward during the approach to SeaTac and shit went sideways. He knew it in the face of everything Death had shown him. He knew it after all of the destruction he'd caused and the glory he'd seen. After everything, his life finally had a direction. A plan. And all it needed was one simple fact in order to work.

He had to live.

Chapter 14

Ethan stepped into the apartment and looked around sheepishly. He was about to get chewed out, but that was the price he had to pay. He couldn't go back, and he'd agreed on that little journey in the first place, so there weren't many options.

"You son of a bitch!!!" was the particularly apt statement that came from the living room as an enraged Arlene came rushing at him, murder in her eyes which had clearly been crying recently. "Where the hell have you been?" She was at him, pushing him back against the now-closed door. The amount of strength she displayed was staggering for someone so small.

"Whoa, whoa, easy girl," Ethan replied, holding his hands back, waiting for the punches to fly. "I'm sorry, I'm *ouch* sorry!" She'd started punching him in the shoulder, looking to do whatever damage she could.

She stepped pack, panting. "Half of the god damned city is out looking for your sorry ass, Ethan! The police and your little cult of followers are all over the place. The media is saying you've committed suicide in a fit of depression! Where the hell have you been?"

Ethan tried with every ounce of strength he had not to smirk. Man, *that* would be one hell of a story, but he didn't think Arlene was up for any of his shit. "Look, I'll explain. I will! Just relax. Let's talk about this." Arlene backed off, clearly waiting for an answer that satisfied her. "So, let's start with the most important thing: I have a cult of followers? How many? Are any of them hot?" She instantly unleashed a small yet efficient punch to his still-sore ribs, winding him.

"Talk!"

"Alright, alright. C'mon, have a seat." He indicated the kitchen table where only a few days before he had sat with Death drinking coffee. She hesitated at first, but eventually agreed, sitting and looking sternly at him, waiting.

He suddenly wished he had a coffee. He'd finally eaten before he got here, knowing what he was likely to face in the coming days, but he'd missed that fine-ass coffee Death had brought. He hoped it was still around. "Alright, so, I'm sorry I fell off the grid. I never meant to worry you. I swear! I never thought you'd fly all the way back here *again* to check on me. I just figured you'd let me get it out of my system and wait for me to get in contact with you."

"I was going to! But Tony called me. He said he'd come home and saw that you'd been here, saw your phone left behind, saw what looked like a couple of dirty cups at the table like you and someone else left in a rush, and wondered if you'd said anything to me about taking off or meeting anyone. I said you were meeting friends from work and that's all I knew of. Did you find some chick from work to hide away with? Were you serious about that photocopy girl?"

"Well, partially, but not the orgy part. Tony called you? Really?"

"Yes. Well, I sorta asked him to keep an eye on you and let me know if anything seemed out of place. So I flew back *again*, and when you were missing for more than a day and your work said you never came in, I got worried. Since you're a celebrity, the police took a special interest in finding you."

God damned Tony; a rat for his own sister. Well played, sis. "Huh. Don't trust me, eh?"

"After what happened and how damned casual you were when I left? Not for a fucking moment."

"Fair enough. Well sorry, no. There were no orgy retreats, sadly."

"Fine, then where were you?"

He'd gone over this story in his head a million times. It still sounded crazy, but he loved her. He had to give her something. "Would you believe me if I said I was out for a job interview?"

"Ha, not for a moment."

"Alright, but this story is going to be pretty hard to believe if you won't buy that." He reached into his tattered jean pocket and produced a particularly slick-looking business card. Arlene snatched it like an overeager toddler with a treat and stared at it.

"Color Sphere Marketing and Consultation?" she said, reading the inscription aloud. "Azreal Pana: President and CEO. What the hell is this?"

"This is the guy who came around offering a job. He was pretty damn convincing, too. He offered to let me get away for a few days while he gave me the grand tour of his office and a place to hide. Put me up in a nice hotel downtown and everything." She looked at him as if every word he said was pure, distilled bullshit. "I'm serious. Google it if you don't believe me." She held her finger up, whipped out her phone, and instantly attempted to call his bluff. When her stern face fell, he knew he'd just earned an ounce of credibility.

"What is this? It looks like a lot of buzz words and corporate jargon." She threw down the phone and the smiling, punchable face of "Azreal Pana" glared back at him, pale, with sun-bleached hair.

"It basically is. They're a marketing company that specializes in making materials for big corporations who have no idea they're being fed a bunch of ideas cooked up by a think-tank to appeal just to them. That's a company secret of course, but I trust you with it. It's a bunch of smart-asses sitting around and cooking up ideas that oblivious companies pay huge money for. Remember those old Pontiac Vibe commercials that made everybody bob their heads to a rhythm? They were so fucking stupid, but everyone was doing it? That was them!"

"What about your phone?"

"Sorry, I couldn't bring it with me. I hadn't accepted the job yet, so it was a security thing. Plus, every time I turn the damn thing on it blows up with media and crazies and all kinds of crap I don't want."

"Yeah, the media is still all over your story. Nothing has distracted them yet, and you've only made it worse by disappearing." She held up the shiny black business card. "A think tank for assholes, you say?"

"You know it. Only the most cynical and spiteful need apply."

"Is the pay good?" She was clearly starting to cool down, though there was still anger there; likely from being so pissed off that her brother had made her fly back and mess up her own life all over again in only a few days. Christ, why was he so lucky to have such a great sister despite the shit they'd been through? Was it their mother that made them so strong together? Probably. It wasn't really something Ethan had dwelled on, but after everything he'd seen and been through, he knew it was true. Not everything about his life was a total shit show. Arlene was proof if it. *Gee, thanks mom. One out of a billion ain't bad.*

"Fantastic. They figured someone with my back-story would be a perfect fit for their team. This guy in particular was a real fan of mine." He indicated the picture on her phone. "Came here, had a quick meeting the morning after you left. Want to try some of the coffee he brought? If it's still here, it's a god damned delight."

Arlene smirked. "It's here. I had some yesterday."

"And?"

"And it's delicious. Tony is buying a crate of the stuff from some place in Canada."

"I know, right! And this stuff is just their regular morning brew. It was a nice place. All kinds of great things to see and crazy ideas flying around."

Arlene relaxed a bit. "You were really at a job interview for the last three days?"

"Arlene, I swear it. I am so sorry you came all the way back here. I should have let you know, but it all just happened so fast, and I was so eager to get away once the media started popping up again." It was true. There was more than a few buzzing around his place right now, but he was able to get inside without them noticing. "I'll make it up to you. I promise. I'll pay you back for your plane ticket and everything once I get back to work or the settlement comes through. I may sell movie rights, too."

"You're damn right you are. I'm obviously going to be played by Anna Kendrick. And you're going to pay me back all of my lost wages with the money you make. I used just about every drop of sympathy and goodwill I could muster to get back out here. When do you start this great new job you put me in a panic over?" She indicated the card again.

It was Ethan's turn to smirk. "I said, 'No'."

"You said what?"

"I said no. The word often associated with yes. Negative. Nyet."

"What? But why? Money? Privacy? Getting paid to be yourself, which is a dick, while sticking it to various 'men'? Making your own way without answering to others? Why the hell would you turn that down?"

Ethan sighed and sat back, resigned to his new fate. "Because I just survived a fucking plane crash. I just put our drugged-out mother in the ground and I never shed a tear about it. I walked back into a life that has no noticeable upside, but I'm not ready to leave this. Not yet."

"Frankly, you're a horrible salesman."

"I know, right? But it's true. I need to get my head straight before I jump into some fancy-ass job like that. Being a ghost with a cult following seems like a great place to start. This is where I want to be. At least for now. Azreal said I'd always have a place there. They have some big project going on soon, and they said they'd really like my help with it. I said I may pop in, but I'm not committing to them completely. Not yet. Everything is still too fresh. I may seem calm and cool, and hell, I feel like I am, but there's also a pretty good chance I'm fucked-up and I can't deal with it all and I'm just ticking along until the crash, you know?"

Arlene sat back as well, and the two Dessier siblings just stared at each other for a moment before Arlene started to smile. After a moment, they were both laughing and hugging with Ethan repeating how sorry he was.

"You know this means I get a bigger piece of that settlement money, right? I mean, once we clear up where you've been and what's been going on with the police and stuff. Fuck the media. They can figure this shit out on their own."

"Fuck the media indeed… Wait, a *bigger* piece? Who said you get any? I was the one in a plane crash!"

"Oh get over it, you baby. You owe me for emotional trauma." Arlene smirked at him. A smirk he knew very well since it mirrored his own so closely. Two healthy peas in a gross pod on a dead plant.

Ethan relented. "Fine. I'll buy you breakfast. I know a few places nearby. But after, that you're on your own."

"I'd say it's negotiable, but breakfast is a good start. Let me get my coat from your room and message some folks that you're ok. If you leave this apartment before I get out of that bedroom, I will hunt you down and slaughter you. And *you* better call the police and let them know you're alright. I'll bet they have a few things for you to fill out and questions to answer."

"Oh I bet they do, but they can wait until after I take my sister to breakfast."

Arlene agreed and she turned around towards his room, the spring back in her step a bit. Curiosity got the better of Ethan, though. "Hey Arlene?"

"What?" she asked, turning back around.

"This is a stupid question, but humor me, ok?" She glared at him suspiciously, but agreed. "What's your favorite memory with Mom? Or even just from our childhood? I've been thinking about it a lot lately, but I was wondering about you, too."

Arlene smirked. "Not much of a contest really. She wasn't exactly the most giving when it comes to happy thoughts and smiley times."

"Tell me about it please, just off the top of your head."

Arlene stood straight, trying to physically show her conviction to the answer. "Mystic Waters. No question. Nothing even comes close. Damn, we all had so much fun that day."

Ethan smiled. "Me too. By a long shot. I just wanted to know."

Arlene nodded respectfully. "I guess we're going to be thinking a lot about that kind of thing in the next little while, aren't we? Oh, well. The families of the one hundred and thirteen of your fellow passengers are going to be doing the same thing. We at least had a warning. What do they have?"

"They get to try to fill those spaces in the universe I guess. Just like us."

She looked at him curiously. It wasn't outside the realm of possibility that Ethan would say something so profound, considering everything that had happened in the last few weeks, so she just left well enough alone and went to get her coat.

The moment she entered the bedroom, Ethan watched the activity outside his window stop again, just like he figured it would. He turned to see Death sitting at the table, looking questioningly at the business card and the phone with his Googled face on it. "Seriously? What the fuck is this crap?"

"This is how I deal with a problem," Ethan replied, holding out his hand and allowing the card to zip through the air to him before it blinked out of existence. "You use guns, I use badly designed business cards."

"I'm sorry, but 'Azreal Pana'? That is the stupidest name I've ever heard."

"Hey, I had to think fast, alright? I needed something believable, but not so perfect that it didn't seem real. She'd have seen right through it. Besides, you look like an Azreal to me."

"That's because I fucking am! You know damn well my Hebrew name, Christian name, my god damned Metis

Indian name! You fucking humans and your insistence on naming things. God, you are such a pain in my ass."

"Well then let's get to it and solve that problem, shall we, now that I know she's ok? Are you ready?"

Death stood up, a hot cup of coffee suddenly appearing in his hand. "One second…" He drank long and deep from the steaming mug. "Ahhhhh, that's the stuff. That's the flavor note I want to go out on."

Ethan walked over, materialized a cup of his own, and held it out. "Cheers. To drugged-out mothers, corporate thinktanks, and hot squirrel sex."

Death smiled, clanking his cup with vigor. "Fuckin' right." They both drank and it was still delicious. When they finished, both cups evaporated.

"Ready to give this a try?" Ethan asked. They were both still uncertain this was going to work. It was new ground.

"I am. It's fucking crazy, but you're the boss. We may tear holes in reality so big they'll make planet-destroying fungal spores look like afternoon tea."

"Maybe, but here we are."

"Here we are indeed." Death held out his hand. "Good luck, kid. This isn't going to be easy."

Ethan grabbed his hand in return and shook heartily. "Don't I know it, but there isn't really a playbook for anyone staying alive while being Death, is there?"

"That is the god's honest truth, sir, but it's so crazy it just might work. I just had to realize that your stubborn self-destructive tendencies were all part and parcel of what the universes need right now. Your mortality is your best, most infuriating weapon." They both smiled as they let their handshake go. "You know, I think I know why it had to be me who recruited you finally."

Ethan raised his eyebrow. "Enlighten me."

"Well, as a squirrel, I was quite possibly the nicest, kindest, most patient creature in that world. The most passive. The most at one with who I was. I enjoyed life and love and all the good things about the world more than any other creature I'd ever met. Of course, I didn't know any of that, because I was a fucking squirrel."

"Ok, but what's that got to do with me?"

"Easy." Death smiled. "I'm probably the only living creature in existence that could put up with all of your shit and not murder you horribly, and then stuff the essence of your being in some god-forsaken pit of nothingness."

"Oh, you do love me. You know I'm keeping my own face, right? I'm not wearing that monstrosity around."

"Hey, you're about to tread on unknown soil, sport. I wouldn't go making demands yet. We have no idea what mortality does to those in the role. Besides, I'm fucking gorgeous." Death stood tall, smirked, and got ready to shuffle off his immortal coil. "Alright. Let's do this. I'm such a sucker for a perfect moment."

"Huh. I never took you for the sentimental type."

"But you take me for a sucker?"

Ethan started to open his mind, as Death had instructed him earlier. It certainly wasn't going to be easy, having the power and omnipresence of being Death, while also maintaining his mortality, but he knew he could do it. If he survived his mother and the *Puget

Plunge (*Patent approved, registered copyright) he could do this, but it was going to be one hell of a learning experience. Soon, the light of the worlds started to fill him, and he felt just like he had on the far-off worlds he'd visited. It was a welcome feeling, and this time it was even more pure. More refined. Soon, as he knew it would, the memory of the nothingness returned as well, starting its war inside him, but he held strong. He knew he could withstand it. He had to. He sure as fuck wasn't going to die. Not after all of this.

"Good luck, Ethan," Death said. "I'll be pulling for you. Just don't go using these bends in the rules to fuck shit up for those of us who care." Ethan didn't respond. "God, I can't wait to be six feet under at last."

"Well," Ethan chimed in, "most graves are actually only four to five feet…"

"Oh dear God, shut up!"

Ethan placed his hand on Death's bare arm, right below his tattoo of a stylized acorn. In an instant, the light began to pour out of him. Ethan was taken aback by the amount that did, filling his apartment and passing through all of his walls. Ethan could feel the light, and he could see the rainbow of color in his head and where each piece needed to go. He could see them all. It was still overwhelming, but nowhere near as much as it was when he saw it through the simple, filtered eyes of a regular person not so long ago. There were gaps and there were problems, but he could fix them. He could fix them all.

And then, Death was gone.

Ethan looked at where he was just a moment before and sighed. "Time to get to work," he said to himself.

"Work? I thought you were buying me breakfast," Arlene's voice came from behind him as the world rushed forward to catch up with itself. Time was an arrow.

"Metaphorical work, Arlene. Putting life back together, dealing with the cops, getting my fucking money, all that jazz."

She nodded and headed for the door after slipping on her shoes. "Good. I like this plan. Ready?"

"Ready," he answered. And, just as Ethan started to walk out of the door, so too did an infinite number of Ethans spread out across the vast expanse of everything, putting lights and colors in their proper place. Death was truly everywhere.

Epilogue

God, he hated this airport. When he was younger, before he got out of that horrible situation he'd found himself in, he used to come through here all the time. He got out of Chicago and its god-forsaken winters and mediocre sports teams and went south, like a smart person would once he had the balls to get out. Far away from do-nothing wives and annoying Cubs fans. Win just *one* World Series in over a hundred years…

He hated having to come through here. He never really regretted what he did, but there was always a chance it would come back to bite him, and being in O'Hare even if it was just for a few hours on a stopover always put him on edge.

He'd just come back from an ice fishing trip with a few old friends who may or may not know his shitty backstory and was resting before boarding at the one stop he had to endure from North Dakota. It was beautiful country up there, but he was glad he could get back to his Florida home and not have to stay up here too long. God, it was cold. He'd gotten soft regarding weather in the seventeen years since he'd left.

It was busy as always here. Moving moving moving. People gotta get places, right? That was the theory. He imagined this was what New York City was like twenty-four hours a day, and if that was true, you could keep it.

He sat and waited as they called out the first groups to be pre-boarded for his flight back to Jacksonville. Almost time to get back. He missed his dog and his bed.

As for his wife? Well...

He had started feeling a bit left of center lately, and this trip was part of the ways he'd devised to get himself righted. He had a doctor's appointment on the books for the next day, and although he'd usually been a decently healthy man, a quick checkup was likely a good idea. He didn't work out or anything, but he stayed fit enough.

"Jacksonville is quite a place, isn't it?" came a sudden and unexpected voice from his right. He hadn't seen anyone sit down, but he was too busy people-watching to really notice.

"I'm sorry?" he said, not really wanting to engage in a conversation but not being able to escape this one without being completely rude all the same.

The speaker was young. Maybe early twenties. He wore a black beanie hat and thick glasses with jet-black frames. Even his coat, a long leather trench coat, was black. In fact, everything was. He didn't look like a mod or a punk or a goth or whatever they called themselves these days, but anything was possible. His shoes were even perfectly black Doc Martins. "Jacksonville. It's a nice place. I've been there a few times, and recently, too. Less tourists. More real Floridites? Floridors? What do they call themselves?"

"Floridians," he answered.

"Lord, that's even worse. Good people, though. You live there?"

Marc Watson

He started to suspect he was about to be sold something. This situation and this kid speaking to him had too many oddities about them to be normal. He tried to play uninterested. "Yeah, almost twenty years now. I love it. Like you said; good people."

The young man nodded. "For sure. You got family there?"

"Wife. Dog. Fridge full of cold beer. All a man needs, really." Why was he still engaging this guy?

"Well said. That, and maybe some kids if you're so inclined. Not that there's anything wrong with the empty-nest lifestyle, either. Just sayin'."

"Yeah, no kids," he answered, not sure why he was so willing to give this guy so much information. He seemed older than his appearance. More worldly. Was he rich? Eccentric? Probably both. "Wife and I never wanted any."

The young man held his hands up. "It's cool, man. I don't judge. Kids are hard. Or at least, I'm told they are. Don't have any myself, either."

The young man reached into an unseen travel bag beside him and pulled out some kind of food wrapped in a paper towel. "Gotta bring our own food these days, right? The prices they charge for a decent meal on these flights are just murder."

"Yeah," he replied, hoping the conversation was going to end soon. He didn't add anything else.

The young man unwrapped his snack and took a few big bites. The man had to admit it smelled pretty good, whatever it was.

181

"Ah, I love muffins. Blueberry are my favorite. You want one? I have extra." He started to reach back around to his bag.

"No! No, thank you," he answered in a rush. "I can't eat blueberries."

"Oh shit, I'm sorry. Am I, like, endangering your life eating this right now, like a peanut allergy or something?" He started to put it away.

"No, no, nothing that bad. I just break out in hives if I eat them. Nothing life-threatening."

The man relaxed and turned back around, continuing to eat his blueberry muffin. "Oh, well that's good I guess. Better than getting all puffy or dying or something." He eventually polished off his muffin and started brushing the crumbs off of his coat. "I've got a place that makes the best damn blueberry muffins you have ever tried. I mean, if you could… But unfortunately, it's all I've got to snack on. It's a shame you can't partake. The lady who makes them is a peach. Well, sometimes."

Satisfied the crumbs had been looked after, he reassembled his travel bag, which the man could see now was also a deep black as he stood up to leave. In fact, he'd swear to it that every piece of this young guy's outfit matched perfectly. That was weird, wasn't it? "Well, gotta move on. Thanks for the chat." The young man started to walk away.

He was shocked he hadn't been given the hard sell or something, but then he was even more surprised that the young man was leaving. "Wait, isn't this your flight? It's just started to board."

The young man turned and readjusted his glasses. Even the shirt under his coat was black. "Ah, sadly no. Even though Jacksonville in March sounds delightful, I've got business elsewhere. I travel around a lot with my job, so I don't get to really settle in anywhere. I didn't mean to startle you when I sat down. You were probably waiting for me to start talking about Jesus or a great timeshare deal or something, right?"

He shrugged. "Well, it had occurred to me…"

The young man waved his hand playfully as if swatting a fly. "Nah, don't worry about it. I just like to sit with people as the world goes by sometimes. It's the only decent human interaction I get some days."

"Oh," he replied, with no answer really satisfactory enough to add to it. It was an odd thing to do, but he supposed it wasn't such a bad thing: to want to reach out to people while they all waited around. "Well, have a good trip, wherever you're going."

The young man took a step back towards him. "You too." He extended his hand and he took it. He figured it was also the polite thing to do. They shook heartily. The young man's grip was strong and confident.

However, as soon as they touched, he couldn't help but feel an odd sensation in the back of his head. Did he know this kid from somewhere? He seemed familiar, but he couldn't place it. He was usually pretty good with faces. Also, on top of the familiarity, there was something else. Something inside himself. As if he was getting tired. He suddenly felt like he really needed a nap. The man kept shaking.

"Hey," he said, "thanks for looking out for me."

He let go and left him sitting there, confused. What was going on? He watched the young man start to walk away, and just before he went out of sight he could see him talking to an airport employee and pointing back at him. He was feeling swimmy now, and he wasn't sure what was happening. He seemed to be blacking out.

Suddenly the airport employee started running towards him, shouting something into her radio. He couldn't hear it, but he could see the people in the area slow down and look at him.

He started to slump over, losing consciousness. Just before he went dark, he saw the young man in black round a corner, not once looking back.

And then, he felt something give deep inside his chest, and just like that he was gone.

91216235R00114

Made in the USA
Columbia, SC
18 March 2018